D1711477

DARKNESS BEGINS

AFTER THE EMP BOOK ONE

HARLEY TATE

DARKNESS BEGINS

A POST-APOCALYPTIC SURVIVAL THRILLER

If the power grid fails, how far will you go to survive?

Madison spends her days tending plants as an agriculture student at the University of California, Davis. She plans to graduate and put those skills to work only a few hours from home in the Central Valley. The sun has always been her friend, until now.

When catastrophe strikes, how prepared will you be?

Tracy starts her morning like any other, kissing her husband Walter goodbye before heading off to work at the local public library. She never expects it to end fleeing for her life in a Suburban full of food and water. Tackling life's daily struggles is one thing, preparing to survive when it all crashes down is another.

The end of the world brings out the best and worst in all of us.

With no communication and no word from the

government, the Sloanes find themselves grappling with the end of the modern world all on their own. Will Madison and her friends have what it takes to make it back to Sacramento and her family? Can Tracy fend off looters and thieves and help her friends and neighbors survive?

The EMP is only the beginning.

Darkness Begins is book one in *After the EMP*, a post-apocalyptic thriller series following the Sloane family and their friends as they attempt to survive after a geomagnetic storm destroys the nation's power grid.

Subscribe to Harley's newsletter and receive an exclusive companion short story, *Darkness Falls*, absolutely free.
www.harleytate.com/subscribe

DAY ONE

CHAPTER ONE

MADISON

University of California, Davis
10:10 a.m.

The bright red fruit peeked out from behind a leaf and Madison smiled. A ripe tomato in the middle of March. She glanced up at the roof of the university's greenhouse and the glass panes streaked from last night's rain.

Staying on campus for spring break meant no house parties with her old friends from high school or tan lines from a trip to the beach, but that suited Madison just fine. She could tend to the plants, work on her research, and have the entire greenhouse to herself for most of the day.

A new song began on the radio and Madison chimed in, belting out the lyrics as she leaned over the nearest row of plants. The plants loved it when she sang.

1

All that carbon dioxide flowing from her lips made for happy little tomatoes.

She started in on the second verse when the radio crackled, cheesy pop turning to nothing but static. Madison reached for the knob, turning it this way and that. Nothing.

That's weird.

She switched to AM, trying to bring in a different station. From the greenhouse location out in the middle of the agricultural fields, she could occasionally pick up a station as far away as the coast or even Nevada. Today she got nothing.

Just the same unending static.

Maybe the batteries need replacing. The radio had to be ancient. Half of the students who came into the greenhouse had never seen a radio with manual dials instead of digital displays. It had stickers all over it from various restaurants and bars and a few political campaigns that happened over a decade ago.

Regardless of its age, the little radio served its purpose. Without it, she would have driven herself mad with the silence of nothing but plants growing.

After switching the radio off, Madison turned back to the task at hand: measuring the growth of her tomatoes. She pulled out her ruler when the door to the greenhouse opened and a familiar voice called out.

"Hey, stranger. Thought I'd find you here."

"Hi, Peyton." Madison eased back on the stool and smiled as her favorite agriculture student sat down beside her. Peyton George might be as unlike her as

2

possible—tall vs. short, broad vs. thin—but he was the best study partner a girl could ask for.

They had been friends ever since Madison accidentally took his chair the first day of class. Three years later, they were de facto siblings and probably closer than the real thing.

Madison glanced at her watch. Peyton wasn't supposed to be here. "Shouldn't you be headed to the airport?"

Instead of answering, Peyton focused on the row of plants in front of him, sticking his fingers in the soil to check the moisture content. As a senior, Peyton didn't need to be in the greenhouse every day. His major research project was in the analysis stage, not data collection.

But he still came to check on Madison and give any advice he could offer. His silence could only mean one thing: he'd fought with his father again.

Madison pushed a little harder. "Doesn't your dad have that big release party tomorrow?"

Peyton scratched at his buzz cut. "Yeah. But I'm not going. I canceled the ticket."

"What? Why?" Madison knew how important the launch of his own record label was to Peyton's father. He had worked for years in the music industry, pulling all-nighters and often missing out on Peyton's childhood. He seemed to care more about his artists than he did his own kid.

Something had to happen. "Your dad's been on your case to go for months. What changed?"

Peyton exhaled. "It's just not my thing. You know

3

that. I left music behind when I came here for school." He pulled out a stool and sat down. "I don't want to follow in his footsteps. He should know that by now."

"But he's your dad. You should go, just to show support."

Peyton snorted. "Like he's supported me? You remember what it was like last year. When I told him I wasn't majoring in business, it was as if I'd confessed to murder. He stopped talking to me for a month, refused to take my calls." He shook his head. "It's only gotten worse."

Madison gave Peyton's arm a squeeze. "Maybe he just needs some time. He'll come around."

"No, he won't."

Peyton sounded so sure, but Madison had her doubts. His dad might not understand the choices Peyton made, but he was still flesh and blood. "Maybe you should—"

"He cut off my funding."

"What?" Madison blinked. "You mean your credit card?"

"No." Peyton shook his head. "He left me that for when I come to my senses and need to book a flight home. He just took all the rest. My tuition, room and board, everything related to school."

Madison reeled. What kind of father would do that? Especially when he had more than enough money to provide for Peyton and a whole host of other kids if he had any. "When?"

"Yesterday, after I told him I wasn't changing my major." Peyton swallowed, his Adam's apple bobbing up and down as he worked to control his emotions. "He told me if I wasn't willing to be a part of the family business, then maybe I shouldn't be part of the family."

"Oh, Peyton. I'm so sorry." Madison reached out, wrapping Peyton up in the tightest hug she could manage. Her arms didn't come close to fitting all the way around him, but she squeezed anyway.

She couldn't imagine what he was going through.

Every time one of her friends talked about their strained or non-existent relationships with their parents, Madison thanked her lucky stars. Sure, her dad might travel half the month as an airline pilot, but he was a good man. And her mom always supported her no matter what. It didn't hurt that they only lived a half an hour's drive away in Sacramento.

She had wanted to go to UC Davis for so many reasons, but between the best agricultural program in the state and being so close to home, it was a no-brainer. The ability to go home on the weekends when she needed a good hug and a stomach full of her mom's banana muffins couldn't be beat.

After another pat on Peyton's back, Madison let him go. "I'm sorry. That sucks."

He nodded. The emotional toll of his father's betrayal cast deep shadows under Peyton's eyes and turned his usual sunny expression into a scowl.

Madison tried to lighten the mood. "I'm supposed to go home on Friday and spend the weekend with my mom. Do you want to come? She'd love to see you."

Peyton managed a mediocre smile. "Will she bake?"

"Any special requests?"

5

His whole face brightened. "I still dream about those little pocket pies she made over Christmas."

"I'll text her and ask. For you, she'll probably go all out and make peach. Ooooh... maybe lemon." She pulled out her phone and typed up a quick message before hitting Send.

The little bar moved across the screen, but after a moment, a red exclamation point popped up. *Not delivered.*

She frowned. *First the radio, now the phones?* "What the heck is going on?" Madison pulled up her favorites and tapped her mom's name. The call wouldn't go through. She glanced up at Peyton. "Do you have service?"

He pulled out his phone and tapped it before holding it up to his ear. "Well... it says I do, but I'm calling you and all I get is the 'unable to complete this call' recording."

Madison reached for the radio and turned it back on. *Still static.* "This happened right before you came in. I can't get any stations."

Peyton looked up at the ceiling. "There's no storm coming through, is there?"

"The sky's blue. Besides, that wouldn't interfere with the AM stations." Madison glanced around, trying to make sense of it. "Something weird is going on."

As the two of them sat there attempting to place calls and get a station on the radio, the door burst open and a frantic Tucker rushed up to them. His black hair stuck up in every direction, his shirt was mis-buttoned, and he looked like he'd just rolled out of bed and straight into a panic attack.

"Where's Brianna? Have you seen her?"

"No."

He tore a hand through his hair. "We need to find her, like yesterday."

Madison held up her hands. "Slow down."

"No. I can't."

"Is there something the matter? Is it her mom? I know she's been sick, but—"

Tucker shook his head so hard he had to have whiplash. "No, it's not that. Well, at least not yet, anyway. We need to prepare. Get supplies. Make a plan." He checked his watch and hissed. "Shit. We don't have enough time. This thing is happening *today*."

Madison glanced at Peyton. He looked every bit as confused as Madison felt. She turned back to Tucker. "What's happening today?"

Tucker didn't hesitate. "The end of the freaking world as we know it. That's what."

CHAPTER TWO

MADISON

University of California, Davis
11:00 a.m.

"You're joking, right?"

"No. I'm not joking. Haven't you seen the alerts?" Tucker paced back and forth in the space between the tables, popping his knuckles and checking his phone nonstop. "They've been going off for almost an hour. It's incredible. Like nothing we've ever seen with modern technology."

Madison held up her hands as she turned to Peyton. "A little help here?"

Peyton set his phone on the counter and walked over to Tucker. He grabbed him by the shoulders, shaking gently until their friend stopped mumbling and made eye contact. "Pretend we didn't spend the last half hour inside your head, Tucker. Start at the beginning."

"Right. Okay." Tucker backed up, rubbing his hand over his face as he collected his thoughts. "How much do you know about space weather?"

"Huh?" Peyton raised an eyebrow. "That's a thing?"

Tucker exhaled. "Madison?"

She shrugged. "I know a little. My dad's been flying over the North Pole for the last few months. He's got the Sacramento to Hong Kong route."

"So you know about solar flares?"

Madison nodded. "They can cause radios to not work at the poles, that sort of thing. Sometimes my dad gets rerouted if the airline thinks he'll lose radio communication on a flight."

"Hello?" Peyton waved his hands in between Madison and Tucker. "There's a guy here who doesn't have a clue what you two are talking about."

"Sorry, man."

"Can you explain—in English instead of your astrophysics major speak—please?"

"I'll try." Tucker pulled up a stool and sat down. "So you know the sun is our light and heat source, right?"

Madison butted in. "He's an agricultural major. Give him a little credit."

Tucker nodded and continued. "Okay, so the sun, being a star, isn't responsible for just light and heat. It's also responsible for space weather. Since it's this giant ball of gases, it basically erupts all the time, spitting out bursts of energy and particles like giant solar burps."

"The sun burps?"

"Sort of." Tucker pulled out his phone brought up a video frozen with what looked like a giant red and yellow ball of fire. "This is a close-up of the sun." He hit play on the video and a bright burst of light erupted from the side of the sun, followed by a giant ball of darker color.

"What was that?"

"A solar flare followed by a Coronal Mass Ejection."

Peyton gave him a look. "English, remember."

Tucker exhaled. "Have you ever seen a cannon fired?"

Peyton glanced at Madison. "Like at a Civil War reenactment?"

She patted him on the arm. "I remember that! We saw it at the history center last year. There was this big flash and then the cannon ball shot out a second later."

"Exactly." Tucker motioned with his hands. "Think of the solar flare—that bright light that erupted first— like the muzzle flash of the cannon. It travels at the speed of light because that's what it is."

"So it gets to Earth in… eight minutes?"

Tucker nodded. "The Coronal Mass Ejection, or CME, is the secondary burst you saw on the video."

"The cannonball?"

"Yes. Basically, it's this big cloud of magnetized particles. It travels through space more slowly. Depending on the size and speed, it reaches Earth in as little as eighteen hours or as many as three days."

When Tucker explained it, everything made sense. But Madison still didn't understand what any of it had to do with space weather or Tucker's freak-out. "So what does a solar flare and CME have to do with today?"

Tucker pulled up another screen on his phone. It was an alert from the Space Weather Prediction Center.

Madison frowned as she read the message. "What's a G5 geomagnetic storm?"

"Only the most extreme space weather event possible."

Peyton leaned forward to get a better look at the screen. "Is it caused by a solar flare or a CME?"

Tucker nodded. "This time, it's both. My phone's set up to get alerts from NOAA, the National Oceanic and Atmospheric Administration. They're the governmental entity that manages the Space Weather Prediction Center. This morning, I got this." He pulled up another screen, showing the notification.

Madison shook her head. "What's an X-50 solar flare? You're losing me, Tucker." She tried not to sound frustrated, but the more she spoke his astrophysics major jargon, the more confused she became. "Just break it down for us. What's going on?"

Tucker shoved his phone in his pocket and looked at them both. "The biggest solar flare we've ever recorded erupted from the sun this morning around 10:00 a.m. Pacific time. It's already caused widespread radio outages, messed-up GPS coordinates, and thrown the cell network into fits since the navigation and time systems aren't accurate."

"A solar flare can do this? But you said they happen all the time."

"They do. But never this big and most of the time, they don't erupt in the direction of Earth."

"Okay." Madison still didn't understand why it was

an emergency. "So we've lost radio and have bad phone reception. So what? When will it come back?"

Tucker paused, his expression turning grim. "If it were just a solar flare, in a few hours. But that's not the worst of it."

Peyton stood up, pacing in front of Tucker. "Come on, man. This isn't a movie. Just tell us what's happening."

"The solar flare was followed immediately by a massive CME like I showed you on the video. This CME will set off a massive geomagnetic storm the likes of which we haven't seen in almost two hundred years."

Madison swallowed. That didn't sound good. "What will it do?"

"What *won't* it do is the better question. If it's as bad as it's looking like from the current data, it'll cause a massive disturbance to our magnetosphere. It could even cause a solar EMP."

Madison perked up. She'd heard about EMPs from her roommate. "Brianna told me about those. They're electromagnetic pulses. But she said they'd be caused by a nuclear attack, not the sun."

Tucker nodded. "There's different types of EMPs. E1, E2, and E3. An E1 is what a nuclear weapon would give off. E3 is what the sun emits. Sometimes we call it a Solar EMP."

"What will it do?"

Tucker swallowed. "Combined with the other geomagnetic effects of the storm, a solar EMP could cause incredible damage. Think widespread loss of power, blackouts, damage to our gas and oil pipelines, disruption to radios and GPS, total destruction of some satellites. We'll even see the northern lights all the way down here."

Peyton stopped pacing. "How long will it last? A few days?"

Tucker didn't answer right away. He glanced at Madison and then back at Peyton. "Worst case scenario, ten years."

"What?!" Ten years without power? That didn't make any sense. She ran through all the statistics she'd learned in her required civics classes. The United States had a current GDP of over sixteen trillion and over a hundred million workers. The energy sector alone had to employ… how many? Millions, at least.

Madison jumped off her stool and grabbed Tucker by the shoulders, practically shaking him unconscious. He had to have lost his mind. This couldn't be real.

"Madison. Stop it!" Peyton wrapped an arm around her middle and pulled her back. "Breathe." He held her, his chest pressing into her back until she stopped fighting.

She sucked in a breath as Peyton let her go. Her head throbbed like it could explode. "You're making this up. It's an early April Fools' joke, right?"

Tucker shook his head. "No. By all accounts, the CME is massive. If it's big enough, the EMP it produces will not only throw the power grid offline, but it can blow up massive transformers all over the country."

"The power company could just replace them."

"It's not that simple." Peyton sat down. "I studied this in my urban planning class." He rubbed the spot beneath his lips as he spoke, the nervous tick making his voice warble. "The big transformers we use in major cities aren't even manufactured in the United States anymore. We've outsourced so much of our manufacturing, most of our infrastructure is foreign-made."

"So there are extras, right?" Madison looked to Peyton for the answer. "No power company would just have the one working transformer. They have to store extras."

Peyton shrugged. "Some might have one or two. But most don't. We're actually critically deficient as a nation in power security. It's one of the massive flaws of our current system. In my class we looked at ways to fund emergency preparedness and planning, but it was virtually impossible."

He pulled out his water bottle and took a sip before continuing. "Power companies can't justify the cost of storing massive transformers that cost millions of dollars for a what-if scenario when they need to spend that money on responding to hurricanes and other current events."

"Here in California it's even worse than in other areas. Our retail energy market is regulated and we have a ton of environmental regulations like the cap and trade system. The electric companies have finite funds."

Madison eased back onto her stool. Nothing Peyton and Tucker were saying made sense. She understood it intellectually, but it didn't seem real. The sun was the source of so many good things: heat and light and the ability to make plants grow. It couldn't also be the source of modern society's downfall.

She turned her attention to the tomato plants, running her fingers over the velvety leaves. "Say all of this is true. That some massive solar storm is coming our way and about to knock out the power. How long do we have to prepare?"

Tucker glanced at his watch. "Seventeen hours and counting."

Madison had been a Girl Scout since she could barely read, a part of 4-H for almost as long, and she'd camped, backpacked, and generally loved being one with nature and the outdoors. She was all about being prepared.

"Is there a chance this is much ado about nothing?"

Tucker wrinkled his nose. "There's always a chance. Maybe the power won't be knocked out all the way. Maybe it'll only impact Canada or South America and not the US."

"But you think this is the real deal?"

"Yeah, I do."

Madison bent down and picked up her backpack before slipping it on her back. "Then let's find Brianna and make a plan. We should be ready."

CHAPTER THREE

TRACY

S<small>ACRAMENTO</small>, CA
   10:10 a.m.

A <small>PILE OF BOOKS FELL INTO THE RETURN BIN AND</small>
Tracy reached for them with a smile. Tuesdays always
started out slow. A few returns, a handful of regulars,
and lots of peace and quiet. She could ease into the day
with a cup of coffee and a perusal of the news before
the three other library employees arrived.

After scanning each book in the return bin, Tracy set
them on a rolling cart for reshelving. Something she'd
get to in the afternoon.

"Hey Mrs. Sloane, how are you this fine morning?"

Tracy glanced up. "Hi, Joe. I'm well. How about
yourself? Is that leg still giving you trouble?"

"Oh, not so much today. It's not raining." Joe
winked, the wrinkles around his eyes crinkling his skin

like tissue paper. The man was in his eighties and walked with a limp, but that didn't stop him from trekking on foot to the library every morning.

"Can I help you find anything?"

Joe leaned against the counter, the red and black plaid of his shirt standing out against the pale wood. "I sure could use your recommendations on a new book. I've read all those Jack Reacher novels. Now I want something a little more… classic."

Tracy nodded. "How about Agatha Christie? She's got more than just the Hercule Poirot series. Ms. Marple definitely counts as a classic."

Joe raised a sagging eyebrow. "Is that what they're calling old these days?"

Tracy laughed. "I wouldn't know, Joe. The things my daughter says, you'd think she'd grown up on Mars." She reached for the computer mouse and clicked open the library catalog. "But if Ms. Marple isn't your thing, I'm sure we can find something. Give me five minutes, okay?"

"I'll be over at the newspapers. Got to stay current, you know." Joe wobbled a bit as he pushed off the counter, his cane taking the brunt of his weight as he maneuvered around the tables between him and the periodicals.

Tracy smiled as she watched him go. He reminded her of her own father who had passed a few years before; neither one would admit to a single ailment, even if the pain made it hard to get around.

She turned toward the computer to search for Joe's next thriller fix when her phone beeped and lit up.

A text from her husband.

Flight is delayed. Possible reroute around the pole due to space weather. Nothing to worry about, just wanted to keep you in the loop. ETA four hours late arriving in Hong Kong. Will let you know when we leave. Love you, Walt.

Her husband always let her know when his schedule changed. It was one of the reasons she never worried about him, despite the ten-hour-plus international fights he'd been flying lately. After twenty years in the military, commercial airlines were a piece of cake.

She typed back a quick reply. *Thanks, hon. Keep me updated. Love you, too.*

Pulling up a page of available thrillers in the branch, she checked a few boxes in the online catalog when her phone buzzed again. Picking it up, she assumed it would be another update from Walter, but it wasn't.

It was from Madison, her daughter.

Tell Dad to come home, too. Tucker says it's going to be bad.

What? It seemed like she'd popped into a conversation in the middle. It didn't make any sense. Why would Walter need to come home? Tracy typed back a quick reply. *What are you talking about? Call me.*

She hit send and waited. The little delivered notice didn't appear. She typed it again and resent. Still nothing.

What is going on? Tracy opened up her contacts and touched her daughter's name. She hated to call during the school day in case she interrupted class, but the text alarmed her.

Tracy held the phone up to her ear, expecting the

sound of a ringing phone. Instead she got a prerecorded message.

"The cellular customer you are trying to reach is unavailable at this time. Please hang up and try your call again."

Pulling the phone away from her ear, Tracy stared at it. If she couldn't reach Madison to get more information, what could she do? After frowning at the screen for a moment, Tracy reopened the text from her daughter and sent another message.

Call me as soon as you can. I can't reach you. Love you.

She went back to the computer, closing the catalog screen before opening the web browser. She scanned the morning's headlines on her favorite news sites.

Suspect arrested in string of robberies.

Dow hits record high.

No rain in sight for the weekend.

Everything seemed normal. She pushed back in her chair, brows dipping low in concentration as she tried to understand her daughter's text.

Madison mentioned Tucker. She tried to remember Madison's friends. Peyton had been to their house a million times, but she hadn't met a Tucker. Who could he be?

At last, she connected the dots. Tucker was her roommate's boyfriend. Tracy didn't know much about him other than he liked the brownies she'd sent home with her daughter last month and he studied astrophysics.

She remembered Madison gushing about how he saved her grades in physics last year.

Tracy exhaled. *Astrophysics*. She didn't even know what that meant. Thankfully, the internet knew everything these days. According to Wikipedia, astrophysics wasn't just astronomy, but the study of the nature of celestial bodies, including the sun, stars, planets, etcetera.

She frowned. What kind of crisis involved space? Aliens? She snorted and typed in another search: *breaking news space sun stars*.

The first hit was a news alert from some official-looking website. The Space Weather Prediction Center.

A giant red warning flashed across the screen.

Solar flare in excess of X-50 emitted at 13:05 EST. Radio and GPS disrupted. Intermittent cellular network and satellite outages may be reported.

Tracy glanced up at the clock. According to the alert, the flare happened about twenty minutes ago. That would explain the lack of cell reception, but she didn't understand what half of the alert said. Solar flares? X-levels?

Walter had mentioned space weather to her before when he'd talked about his intercontinental flights over the North Pole, but she'd never had the need to understand more than the most basic of details. Now she wished she'd paid more attention.

She picked up her phone and brought up her husband's text. *Space weather delays*. But he'd said there wasn't anything to worry about. Madison seemed almost panicked. Which was it? Nothing to worry about or cause to freak out?

She chewed on her cheek as she thought it over, staring at the computer screen, but not really seeing it.

"Run out of ideas already? Or are thrillers that popular these days?" Joe had made his way back to the front desk and stood in front of Tracy, waiting. She hadn't even noticed his approach.

"I'm sorry Mr. Travers, I haven't had a chance to find those titles."

Joe nodded. "Maybe tomorrow, then." He started to turn away when Tracy stopped him. She knew it was a long shot, but what other options did she have? "You used to work for a satellite company, right Joe?"

"Yes, ma'am." He turned back toward the desk. "One of the best electrical engineers ViaComm ever had."

Tracy thanked her lucky stars for remembering that tidbit of knowledge. "You wouldn't know anything about space weather, would you?"

"Not for my job."

Tracy's hopes plummeted, but Joe smiled. His blue eyes shone as he spoke again. "It is one of my hobbies, though."

Thank goodness. Tracy pushed the computer screen his way. "Do you know anything about solar flares? Is this bad?"

Joe squinted as he stepped closer, his hand coming up to adjust his glasses as he read the screen. He squinted and pointed a shaky finger at the display. "My vision isn't what it used to be. Can you pull up the details there, please?"

Tracy complied. A window popped up with photos of what looked like a massive explosion of light erupting from the sun, followed by what looked like a whoosh of something. "What is that?"

Joe stepped closer, using the desktop instead of his cane for support. "See that right there?" He motioned to the explosion. "That's a solar flare followed by a CME."

"A what?"

"A Coronal Mass Ejection."

"What's that?"

Instead of answering, Joe kept his eyes trained on the screen, reading over the details beneath the photos.

"Joe?"

At last, he turned to her, the pale wrinkles of his face turning ashen as he spoke. "Your daughter's at UC Davis, right?"

Tracy nodded past the lump in her throat.

"Tell her to come home. You'll need to stick together."

"Why? What's going on?"

Joe wiped at the corners of his mouth with his knobby fingers. "If it's what I think it is, all hell's about to break loose."

CHAPTER FOUR

TRACY

Sacramento, CA
10:45 a.m.

She leaned back in her chair, awestruck by the information Joe possessed. The man was a walking encyclopedia of space knowledge. Thanks to him, she'd learned all about solar flares and CMEs and the effect geomagnetic storms could have on Earth.

"I still can't believe no one talks about this stuff. Where are the alerts in the media? Why hasn't anyone said anything?"

Joe sipped the coffee Tracy had made for him before answering. "It isn't real to a lot of people, I guess. We haven't had a massive geomagnetic storm that knocked power out for more than a few hours in our lifetimes. The last major event that caused any sort of panic was in the 1800s."

"What happened?"

"The Carrington Event is the largest geomagnetic storm ever recorded. It caused the aurora borealis to be seen as far south as the Caribbean, telegraph systems all over the world failed and threw sparks or gave the operators electric shocks."

"When was this?"

Joe stifled a cough before continuing. "It was 1859. Some telegraph operators even reported the ability to send telegraphs after disconnecting their power supplies."

"Incredible."

Joe nodded. "But today the same event would be catastrophic. Look at all the electronics we rely on now. Computers are in our phones, our cars. My daughter even controls the lights to her house with an app."

Tracy agreed. The reliance on advanced computers had changed so much since she was a kid. "I remember my brother had a Commodore 64. All I thought it was good for was playing video games."

"Now even our economy is controlled by computers."

"But you said the thing at greatest risk is the power grid."

"I did."

"So maybe it won't be catastrophic. We can rebuild the power lines."

"But we rely on electricity for everything. All those computers and electronics take power to run. Without it…"

Tracy thought about the last time she'd been without

power for an extended length of time. A few years ago, torrential rains had pushed through the area, causing localized flooding. Their home wasn't in the water's path, but a levee broke in the neighborhood next door and the local creek jumped its banks.

The power company shut down the power as a precaution. It took four days to turn back on. By then, all the food in her fridge had gone bad, she had run out of wood for the fireplace, and had been on the verge of moving to a hotel.

What would happen if four days turned into years? Joe explained the science, but it still didn't seem possible. Tracy leaned back in her chair. "This is a lot to process."

"It is." Joe pushed himself up to stand, grabbing ahold of his cane as he slid his chair in. "Thanks for the coffee. I'm sure I've taken up enough of your time."

Tracy smiled. "I always have time for my best library patrons."

"Hi Tracy." Her coworker's voice interrupted her train of thought. "How's the prep for the tax seminar coming? Doesn't that start at eleven thirty?"

Oh, no. Tracy glanced at the clock. 11:25. She had five minutes to prep for the seminar.

Wanda, the head afternoon librarian, stood at the desk, a concerned smile on her face. "Everything all right?" She pushed her glasses up her nose and waited.

"Yep. Just lost track of time. I'll get it set up right away." Tracy reached for Joe and gave his hand a pat. "Thank you, Joe. Hopefully this will all amount to nothing and I'll see you here tomorrow morning just like always."

"Whatever happens, Mrs. Sloane, it's always better to be ready. Remember that."

Tracy nodded and watched him walk toward the front door, the limp hitching every step. *If the power stays out, I'm checking on Joe.* Tracy might have relied on Joe this morning, but she knew he wouldn't be able to survive on his own for long.

The man could barely walk. He couldn't live in a world without power.

"Tracy? The meeting?"

"Coming!" Tracy pushed the thoughts of space weather and her family out of her mind and picked up the stack of tax forms. She had a job to do until four that afternoon. Until then, she needed to focus.

Preparing for the unknown could wait a bit longer.

* * *

Sacramento, CA
2:05 p.m.

THE DOOR TO THE SUBURBAN SHUT WITH A SOLID thud and Tracy took a deep breath for the first time all afternoon. Between the tax seminar, setting up a computer-training class, and scanning the news headlines every chance she could, Tracy hadn't sat down since Joe said goodbye.

She had texted her daughter a million times and called a few, but she had only received one more text:

Be careful, Mom.

That's all it said.

Tracy didn't know if Madison was on her way home, safely tucked in her dorm room on campus, or running around Davis freaking out. She hoped she'd done the sensible thing and decided to stay put.

The college had excellent security and a full staff. Madison would be safe there. At least for a while.

Madison was a resourceful young woman. She might be only nineteen years old, but she knew how to take care of herself. It was Walter that Tracy worried about more.

He hadn't updated her on the flight. Not a single text or call since that first notification all those hours ago. If he was up in the air when the CME hit, Tracy didn't know what would happen. Would the plane drop from the sky? Lose navigation and radio?

If the airports all lost power, how would he land?

She tried not to worry. Walter was a grown man. He had always taken care of their family and kept them safe. Even if the worst happened, he would find a way back home. Tracy just had to have faith.

She started the engine of the SUV and pulled out of the library parking space. Thank goodness Wanda let her leave work two hours early. If Joe was right, then she needed to stock up while she still could. A litany of items ran through her mind. Groceries. Paper products. Emergency supplies and first aid.

When Madison was little, Tracy always kept a fully stocked pantry with multiple packages of everything she needed just so she didn't have to run to the store. She'd even gone through a crazy couponing phase, stocking up on everything from soap to shampoo to cereal. They'd turned their spare bedroom into a veritable grocery store stockroom.

But since Madison left for college, Tracy and Walter sold their large family home and downsized. Their two-bedroom, one bath, little bungalow barely had enough room for a two-cabinet pantry. There simply wasn't enough space for extras.

The things she loved about their new home when they bought it all seemed so trivial now. The small footprint, easy-to-care-for yard, and quiet neighborhood with a park in the middle, didn't mean a thing if in a handful of hours life as they knew it took a nosedive.

She thought of her neighbors. The Smiths next door had a toddler and a baby on the way. The Rodgers across the street worked for the city school district and ordered delivery almost every night. No one she knew would be prepared for something like this. How much food would they have on hand? What type of supplies?

How long would the neighborhood stay civil and friendly if the power never came back on? Desperation made people do terrible things. She knew that firsthand.

Tracy pulled into the local grocery store parking lot. It didn't seem any busier than a typical Tuesday afternoon. Stepping out of the SUV, she slung her purse over her shoulder and headed inside.

In case Madison and Walter made it home, she needed to buy enough food for all of them. Things that would last. If nothing happened, she could always donate the extra to the food bank. It was something she'd been doing for years.

After pulling a cart out of the row, Tracy headed inside the store. If she was lucky, no one she knew would be shopping and she could be in and out without anyone questioning her. Explaining why she had a cart full of enough food to feed an army wasn't something she knew how to do.

Bypassing the produce, Tracy headed straight to the bottled water and sports drinks. She piled cases of both in the bottom of her cart, filling the entire space. It wasn't nearly enough.

She glanced up and down the aisle. No one was there. Why weren't people freaking out? Did they simply not know? Was she blowing it all out of proportion?

After stacking another case of water inside her cart, she headed to the canned goods. Chicken and tuna and beans all went into her cart along with packets of already-cooked rice and cans of ravioli and meatballs.

She smiled with a mix of regret and nostalgia. Spaghettios straight from the can had been a good meal when she was a kid. It sure beat nothing. Now it might keep her family fed when the world fell down around them.

The cart already teemed with food, but Tracy wasn't close to done. She needed peanut butter and crackers. Nuts and protein bars. Anything that could keep in the pantry without refrigeration.

She needed a trip to Costco.

"Hey, Tracy. Is that you?"

Oh, no. She turned to see a woman walking down the

aisle with a handheld shopping basket and a fancy coffee.

"It's Melanie, from Loma Blanco High. Our daughters were in the same class."

"Oh, right. Your daughter is Kristie, right?"

Melanie nodded, her ponytail bobbing behind her. "Are you getting ready for a party or something? That's a lot of tuna… and Gatorade. Wow."

Tracy swallowed. Should she tell her the truth? What if it all turned out to be nothing? Would this woman she barely knew think she'd gone off the deep end? All she remembered about her daughter was that Madison didn't care for her. Something about having more clothes than sense.

She hedged. "I donate a lot to the food bank. They can always use canned goods."

"How thoughtful of you. Did you know I'm on the board of the Children's Hospital? We do a fundraiser every year. It's more of a gala type thing, but you get the idea."

Tracy didn't. Not at all. She just wanted to get out of the store, load up her Suburban and get over to Costco before rush hour. She smiled. "I'm sure it's wonderful. How's Kristie?"

Melanie beamed. "In Cancun. Spring break only comes once a year, you know. How about Madison? Is she off somewhere fun? Hawaii, maybe?"

"She's back at school, working."

"Oh." Melanie sipped her coffee. "Good for her, being industrious and all."

Tracy couldn't stand it another minute. She'd made

enough small talk. "It's been good talking to you, but if you don't mind, I'm kind of in a hurry."

"Of course. All those donations… you probably want to get those to the food bank right away."

"Something like that. Nice to see you, Melanie."

"You, too!" Melanie waved as Tracy pushed the cart down the aisle toward the checkout. There were still a million more things to get, but she had to get out of her local supermarket and into a big box store. No one would question her motives there.

Lying wasn't something Tracy made a habit of, but what could she do? Melanie didn't strike her as the type to take space weather seriously. If she did tell her, the woman was liable to either blow it off or panic.

Tracy slowed the cart to a stop in the checkout aisle and took a deep breath. Panic was never a good thing. She needed to remember that.

CHAPTER FIVE

MADISON

University of California, Davis

12:00 p.m.

"What about all the plants? The research? If we lose power, the automatic sprinklers won't turn on."

Peyton scratched his head. "We could water everything now. Change the timers to go off early. It would buy us some time."

"Guys, come on. We can't stand around here worrying about the agriculture department. We need to find Brianna and get out of here."

"But half of these plants are food, Tucker. What if we need it?"

He glanced around at the rows of tomatoes and peppers. "How long will this all last without water?"

Madison bit her lip as she thought it over. "If we

water them extra right now, maybe a week. Longer if it's not too hot."

Tucker frowned. "Fine. Water them, but do it quick. We need to get going."

Peyton headed to the back of the greenhouse where the sprinkler controls were located while Madison began to open up the sprinkler heads to full spray.

"Can you twist that row to full on?" She motioned to the next row over and Tucker complied, opening up each sprinkler to the max it could go.

Peyton walked back into the room as Madison and Tucker finished. "I reprogrammed the controls." He rubbed the back of his neck as he glanced around. "If this is all one big false alarm, we're ruining months of research for nothing. We could get expelled over this."

Madison looked at Tucker. "You're sure this is the real thing? We're not overreacting?"

"In less than twenty-four hours, there won't be an agricultural program to come back to." Tucker reached for his backpack and slung it over his shoulder. "If you're done, let's go."

The three of them filed out of the greenhouse and Madison shielded her eyes from the bright noon sun. It seemed like any other day. The sun still shone; the birds still sat on the tree branches chirping among the new spring leaves.

How could anything bad be about to happen? She glanced back at the greenhouse. If they were really on the verge of a massive, countrywide blackout like Tucker claimed, she might never be back here.

"Hold on, guys. I need to grab something." Madison

rushed back inside, running down the row of plants, until she stopped in front of her work station. She grabbed the little portable radio she'd been listening to that morning and shoved it in her backpack.

It ran on batteries. If anyone was out broadcasting after tonight, she wanted to hear them.

A half an hour later, they made it back to the dorm and to the room she shared with Brianna.

"It's about time the three of you showed up. We should have been on the road an hour ago." Her roommate's brash scolding made Madison smile. Leave it to Brianna to already have one foot out the door.

"Did you get my texts?" Tucker headed straight for Brianna, wrapping her up in a quick hug before pulling back.

"Yeah. I tried to respond, but my phone wouldn't work." Her brown eyes practically sparkled. "This is it, isn't it?"

"Could be."

"Then we shouldn't waste any more time. We need to load up all we can, get gas, and get on the road. The cabin's a three-hour drive from here."

Brianna cinched the top of her hiking pack while she shoved the contents down with her other hand. The pack was stuffed to the gills.

Madison couldn't believe Brianna had everything together. It had only been a couple of hours. "What's in there? It looks like you've packed everything but our bathroom sink."

Brianna pulled her curly blonde hair back into a low ponytail and slipped on a hoodie. "My dad always told

34

me something like this would happen. It's why he worked so hard to buy the place up in the mountains and why he's stashed so many supplies up there. I always thought he was crazy, but he was right."

Madison exhaled. She knew all about Brianna's prepper dad and the outlandish theories he had about the end of the world. "First your dad thought Y2K was going to kill all the computers, then it was some Mayan prophecy in 2012, now it's terrorists with nuclear bombs. This isn't any of that, Brianna. It's the sun."

"So?" Brianna glanced around the room. "What's the difference, really? Whether it's economic collapse or a solar EMP or World War III, it's all the same. Everything we know about life is going to change. All the things we take for granted…" She pointed at Madison's cell phone in her hand and the laptop computer sitting on the desk. "All of it's going to be worthless without power. We might as well be pre-Industrial Revolution."

Peyton snorted. "You really think we're going all Dark Ages? Just because the power goes out?"

Tucker spoke up. "If this is as bad as I think it will be, yeah. It will take years to get the grid back up. Can we really hold on that long? What if it's not just North America that's hit? What if it's the whole Earth? Things will devolve pretty darn quick."

Madison thought about the cheesy reality shows she used to watch on TV. A bunch of people thrown on a deserted island with nothing but their wits. It didn't take long for factions to form and fights to break out.

Add in guns and hunger, and Brianna had a point.

She slumped onto the edge of her bed. "What if we wait until tomorrow? We could get ready, but just stay here and wait it out. It could all amount to nothing."

Brianna rolled her eyes. "And if it doesn't? You really want to be stuck in Davis when my family's got a place that can take care of us for months, if not years?"

Peyton came over and sat beside Madison, slipping his arm around her shoulder. His green eyes held as much fear and uncertainty as her own. "If it turns out to be a false alarm, we can just come back. But shouldn't we be proactive?"

Madison couldn't believe the four of them were even having this conversation. "What about the other people on campus? Why isn't anyone else freaking out?"

"Haven't you noticed it's like a ghost town around here? Almost everyone is on vacation. With the dining hall closed and most of campus shut down, there isn't anyone left to cause a panic."

Peyton had a point. It had been quiet. They were the only two people tending to the greenhouse and apart from Brianna and Tucker, Madison hadn't seen more than a handful of other students. Teachers and staff were all home with their families.

Brianna picked up her pack and slipped it on before buckling the belt in front. "Tucker and I are leaving ASAP. You two should come with us. We've got space."

Madison shook her head. "I can't. I've got to get to my mom."

"What about you, Peyton?"

"I'm going with Madison. If this is nothing, I've got dibs on Mrs. Sloane's peach pie."

Brianna chewed on her lip. "Is your mom at home?"

Madison nodded.

"How are you planning to get there? You don't have a car."

Madison shrugged. "The bus. It shouldn't take too long. I've done it before."

"Don't take the bus. You could get stuck halfway there." Brianna glanced at Tucker. He nodded. "We'll take you."

"No!" Madison looked up, shaking her head. "I can't ask you to do that. You've got family waiting for you."

Her roommate smiled. "You're family, too. Besides, Sacramento's on the way to Truckee. If we leave now we can stop for gas, load up on supplies, and still make it to your mom's place before traffic sets in."

Madison thought it over. Hitching a ride with Brianna meant she'd be sure to get home before the CME reached Earth's atmosphere. But she'd be putting Brianna and Tucker at risk. They should be worrying about their drive upstate, not whether Madison and Peyton made it to Sacramento.

She walked over to her desk and fished around in the drawer before pulling out a small pencil box. She opened it up and handed a wad of cash to Brianna. Madison always kept a stash of cash in case of emergencies. This definitely qualified. "If you're taking us, then I'm buying supplies. It's the least I can do."

Her roommate took the money with a grin. "Deal. Now let's get the hell out of here."

CHAPTER SIX

MADISON

Davis, CA
  1:00 p.m.

Madison stood in the middle of the largest sporting goods store in town, unsure where to even begin. After filling up the tank of Brianna's Wrangler, they had headed straight there.

It still seemed like overkill. She leaned toward Brianna. "I thought your parents were totally stocked. Why are we shopping? Shouldn't we just get on the road?"

The distance between her and her mom made Madison nervous. She just wanted to get home, lock the doors, and relax, not pile a cart full of camping gear.

Brianna frowned, her big brown eyes intense as she stared at Madison. "Haven't you listened to anything I've said?" She waved at the display of sleeping bags in front of them. "You really think any of this will be here in a few days? What if we have to bug out? What if we don't make it to the cabin? We need to be prepared to be on our own."

Madison shook her head. "Even if it's as bad as Tucker says, it's just a blackout. We've all lived through those before."

"Not for a decade." Tucker stopped beside her, a sleeping bag under each arm. "Once people figure out this isn't a temporary thing, you really think they'll wait in line for these?"

He waggled the bags before dumping them in a cart. "Think about it. No electricity means no central heat, no microwaves, no electric stoves. If we don't have ways to stay warm and cook food without power, we won't survive very long."

Brianna agreed. "Think about all the people we know who don't have more than a few days' worth of food. You've seen the refrigerators on campus. Half of them only have beer and ketchup."

"Expired ketchup." Peyton added another two sleeping bags to the cart and pointed at the cold-weather gear. "You should grab a jacket. Maybe some clothes. Something you can wear for a while."

"Cargo pockets. Look for lots of pockets." Brianna patted the side of her pants. "I can put ammo or a knife or first aid supplies in here and not even notice it."

"Ammo?" Madison's brain must have misfired. She couldn't have heard Brianna right. "For what? Hunting?"

"Yeah, but defense, too. If things go south, we'll need to protect ourselves."

It was like someone had swooped down and taken all of her friends and replaced them with crazy militia members convinced the end of the world was just around the corner. "You're overreacting. All three of you."

Brianna shook her head and headed toward the food section. "Keep telling yourself that and you'll starve or get shot before the month is over."

Madison's mouth fell open and she stood there, gawking as Brianna and Tucker disappeared around the corner of an aisle.

"She's got a flair for the dramatic, I'll give you that, but you should listen to Brianna. It makes sense if you think about it."

"Only if you believe the worst of people."

Peyton snorted. "Guess I have more experience with that than you do."

Without another word Peyton walked away, headed toward the hunting section. Madison stood alone, feeling like the only one of her friends who hadn't completely lost her mind. She picked at a nail as she thought about Peyton's comment. He was right.

Between his non-existent mother and jerk of a father, Peyton had seen the worst in people. Madison couldn't say the same. Her parents had always been there for her, supporting her no matter what. Did that mean she was sheltered?

Was she wrong in thinking most of humanity wouldn't devolve into petty criminals? The Girl Scout motto popped into her head: "Be prepared." It wasn't enough to be willing to help out. Ever since she had been a Brownie, her troop leaders explained that a Girl Scout needed to not just be willing to help, but to know how.

That applied even more so in an emergency. She couldn't help people if she wasn't prepared. Maybe she didn't agree with her friends' dire outlook on society, but she understood the desire to be prepared. It wasn't overreacting or putting herself ahead of others.

Stocking up on supplies now meant she could do more to help those in need later when it really mattered. She didn't have to hunker down in some fortified cabin in the woods like a hoarder. She could use her skills to support others who hadn't thought this far ahead.

Madison put the last of her hesitations behind her and pulled out her phone. She tried to call her mom, but only got the same recording she'd heard a hundred times that day: *All circuits are bust now, please try your call again*. With a frown, Madison sent her mother another text:

I'm on the way home. Stay safe. I'll be there soon.

She didn't know if it would ever be delivered, but she needed to try. After shoving her phone in her back pocket, Madison headed to the cold-weather gear. She needed a winter coat and a good pair of boots to start.

Half an hour later, she tracked down Peyton in the firearms department, her arms already tired from lugging a parka, boots, gloves, pants, and as much other clothing as she could carry, across the store. She dumped it all in his cart and exhaled. "I'm as ready for a hike in the mountains in the dead of winter as I'll ever be. A bunch of it was on clearance too."

"Great." Peyton didn't even look up. His eyes were trained on the case of handguns in front of him.

"What are you doing?"

"Buying a gun."

"How? Are you planning on coming back in a couple weeks?"

Peyton glanced up at Madison with a confused expression when a clerk appeared.

"Can I help you?" The man appeared to be a little younger than her dad, mid-forties most likely, with a haircut that screamed military. The tattoo peeking out from under his uniform polo could have been a globe and anchor. Marine Corps.

Madison smiled as he glanced at her. If the world weren't about to end, this would be fun.

Peyton pointed at a handgun in the case. "I'd like to buy this one, please."

The clerk raised an eyebrow and Madison bit her cheek to keep from laughing. Peyton had no idea about the gun laws in California. The closest he'd ever been to a handgun was standing next to a security guard at one of his dad's music launch parties.

Madison had grown up target shooting with her dad and knew the laws in California were only getting tighter. Brianna had complained more than once about the unfairness of it all every time a new law was passed.

After a moment, the clerk nodded. "Okay. I'll need

your driver's license, proof of age, proof of residency, and your Firearms Safety Certificate." He pulled out a stack of papers from under the counter. "Then you'll need to fill out this form. If everything checks out, we can do the safe handling demonstration."

Peyton's eyes almost crossed. "Wait a second. I don't even know what half of that means. Can you start again?"

The clerk flashed one of those smiles that said he'd been there a million times before, but he obliged. "First time, huh?"

Peyton nodded.

"All right. First, you have to be twenty-one to purchase a handgun. From the looks of the pair of you, you're probably cutting that a little close. It's eighteen to buy a shotgun or a rifle."

Peyton glanced up at the wall of shotguns behind the clerk.

"If you are twenty-one and still want a handgun, I'll need proof of residency. So something like a utility bill with your name on it or a lease."

Peyton pulled out his wallet and fished his driver's license out, but the clerk waved him off.

"That's not enough. It has to be something else."

Madison could feel the tension rolling off Peyton in waves. He gritted out a question. "What next?"

"You need a Firearms Safety Certificate."

"How do I get that?"

The clerk pulled out a pamphlet and what looked like a multiple choice test. "You'll need to study and take this test. Thirty questions, twenty-three correct is passing."

"Are you serious?"

"Yep."

Peyton's shoulders sagged. "Then what?"

"Then you fill out the application, I take your thumbprint, and you perform a safe handling demonstration. A certified instructor will have to walk you through the safe handling instructions and you sign a statement saying you completed them."

"Is that it?"

"Nope. Even if you do all that, you still have to wait ten days before you can pick it up."

Peyton huffed, angry words slipping out almost beneath his breath. "This is bullshit."

The clerk half-laughed. "Tell me about it. The legislature has really gone overboard if you ask me. I don't even know why we still sell firearms in this store to be honest. Now with all the new laws that just passed, we probably won't be selling ammo either."

Madison tilted her head. "What new laws?"

"Not only do we have to have a license to sell ammo now, but anyone who wants to buy ammo has to have a four-year permit that requires a background check to get."

"You're joking."

"I wish. But that's not even the half of it. They've also completely changed the definition of assault rifles and made it illegal to own a magazine holding more than ten rounds. If you get caught with one now, the government confiscates it and you have to a pay a fine."

"What? That's crazy!" Madison thought about Brianna and her parents. "What about all the people who bought them before the law was passed?"

The clerk shook his head. "They have to either remove it from California, sell it to a licensed dealer, or turn it over to the police."

Madison couldn't believe it. "Why didn't we hear about these new laws when they were up for vote?"

The clerk shrugged. "You did. You just weren't paying attention. The politicians who supported them made it sound like all it would do was take dangerous weapons off the streets, not make it impossible for mom and pop shops to sell guns and ammo or make it a crime to own something that the Constitution says you can."

Peyton leaned back, his palms flat on the counter to keep from falling over. "This is crazy, man. How do you keep all the laws straight?"

"If I don't, I can go to jail. Gives me a pretty good incentive."

Madison patted Peyton on the arm. "We should get going. You're not buying guns or ammo today."

"Guess not." He held out his hand and the clerk shook it. "Thanks for the info."

"Anytime."

Peyton turned to Madison as she grabbed the cart handle. "Let's find Brianna and get out of here. I don't want to be out on the roads when people start figuring out what's going on. Especially not without a gun."

Madison nodded. Part of her was glad Peyton couldn't buy one, since he didn't know the first thing about gun safety or how to even shoot one. But she wouldn't have minded a rifle or a shotgun of her own just in case.

Pushing the cart toward checkout, Madison spotted Brianna and Tucker, their own cart loaded up with everything from propane and a camping stove to freeze dried food and a water filtration system. Between the two carts, they were as prepared as four college kids could be.

Brianna and Tucker waited until Madison pushed her cart up to meet them. "Ready?"

She nodded. "One question, how are we going to pay for all this? I gave you my emergency cash, but it's not nearly enough."

"Don't worry, I've got it." Peyton stepped forward, shiny black Amex in his hand. "My dad didn't cancel the credit card, remember?"

Madison exhaled. "Keep the receipt. I'll pay him back later."

"*Pfft*. You will not. He owes me. Besides, after tomorrow, money's not going to be worth a damn thing."

"Assuming anything actually happens."

"It's happening, Madison. The sooner you come to terms with it, the better." Brianna pushed her cart up behind Peyton's in line. Tucker held back and waited for Madison.

"I know you don't think it's as bad as they do, but NOAA doesn't lie. They wouldn't have sent out an alert if it wasn't serious."

Madison scrunched up her nose. "Why haven't you gotten any more? Why hasn't the government come out and said something?" She glanced at her watch. "It's three o'clock in the afternoon. The first alert went out hours ago."

Tucker scratched at his moppy black hair. "I don't know. But phones haven't been working right. The alert system could be down, too."

"Maybe." Madison fidgeted in line, her unease over the whole day growing by the minute. They'd wasted too much time in the sporting goods store. They needed to get out of there and get to her mom's house. Soon.

Peyton's turn in line finally came and he stepped up to the counter. "Hi. I've got two carts to check out, please."

The cashier glanced first at the carts and then at Madison and Tucker. "That's a lot of stuff. You sure you can pay for all of it?"

Peyton flashed the credit card. "Yeah, I'm sure."

"I'll need to see some ID. And I'll have to use the manual imprinter. Our credit card processing isn't working."

Peyton stacked the first set of supplies on the counter. "Whatever works."

After what seemed like forever, they finished. Peyton and Madison took hold of the carts loaded up with supplies while Brianna held the mile-long receipt.

"You sure your dad's okay with this?"

"I'm sure that right now I don't care." Peyton pushed his cart a little harder, jumping up onto the bottom rail as it sailed through the parking lot. "Race you to the car."

Madison smiled and gave her cart a shove. "You're on!"

The two of them careened to a halt inches from the back of Brianna's Jeep as a series of beeps sounded through the parking lot.

Madison pulled out her phone and Peyton did the same.

The screen lit up with something she'd never seen before: Emergency Presidential Alert.

She glanced up at Peyton. "Are you getting this?"

He nodded as Brianna and Tucker caught up to them. "What's going on?"

"Check your phones. We're getting an alert."

Madison's friends pulled out their phones and the four of them stood in the parking lot staring at their screens as another message popped up.

Emergency Presidential Alert.
Severe Space Weather Warning in this area until 08:00 AM PST.
Take Shelter Now. Dusk to Dawn Curfew in Effect.

Madison reread the message four times before she glanced up at her friends. Tucker was right. Something big was about to happen and they were still thirty miles from her mom.

Brianna beeped her car unlocked. "Everybody load up. Shit's about to get real."

CHAPTER SEVEN

TRACY

Sacramento, CA
3:30 p.m.

There wasn't enough room in the Suburban for all the supplies Tracy needed. Her brows knit in a scowl as she stared at the cases of water and Gatorade already loaded up on the flatbed. She needed a whole convoy full of water and food if the growing fear in her gut was anything to go by.

People milled around her, all typical weekday afternoon shoppers. A man with a flatbed like her own, full of industrial paper towels and cleaning supplies. A woman with three little kids and a cart full of snack foods and diapers.

Was she the only person in the city freaking out? Was this all in her imagination?

Joe had taken it seriously. He'd told her the risks of an extreme geomagnetic storm. Her husband had talked about space weather before.

Tracy pulled out her phone and tried her husband. Instead of ringing, she received the same network congestion message that plagued her all morning: *All circuits are busy, please try your call again.*

She opened text messages and scrolled through them again. *Where are you, Walt?*

Her concern over the safety of both her husband and her daughter was starting to take its toll. She'd downed a soda and two ibuprofen earlier, but it hadn't made a dent in the tension headache behind her eyes.

If she couldn't reach them, all she could do was prepare for the worst and hope they either stayed put somewhere safe or made it home in one piece. She wouldn't be much good to anyone if she didn't finish this trip and get back to the house.

Pushing the flatbed down the aisle, Tracy tried to focus. What would they need if the power stayed out? Water. Paper products. A way to dispose of trash. Food, food, and more food.

She grabbed a couple boxes of heavy-duty black trash bags, paper plates, and as many paper towels as she could fit in the truck. Then it was on to boxes of granola bars and jerky. As she headed toward checkout a display of protein powder caught her eye. She grabbed a few canisters as a young woman with a baby strapped to her chest stopped next to her.

The woman couldn't have been older than twenty-five. She reached for a case of formula, but the baby only got in the way.

"Here, I can help." Tracy pulled the case off the stack and set it in the woman's cart.

"Thank you. She screams if I put her in the basket."

Tracy smiled. It had been so long since Madison was that little. She almost didn't remember what babies were like. "What's her name?"

"Savannah. We named her after our hometown."

"She's beautiful."

"Thank you."

Tracy turned to go when the woman touched her arm. "Have you heard? About the weather?"

"You mean the CME?"

The woman nodded. "Is it as bad as they say? Are we really going to lose power?"

Tracy looked down at Savannah blowing bubbles and kicking her chubby little legs. She had the pinkest cheeks Tracy had ever seen. "I wish I knew."

"Me too." The woman bit her lip and glanced back at the formula. "Could you help me with a few more cases?"

"Of course." Tracy loaded four more cases into the woman's cart while the baby just cooed and giggled. "Anything else?"

"No, I think that's it. Thank you."

Tracy nodded. "If I were you, I'd get some water, too. And some nonperishable food. Just in case."

"Right." The woman looked down at her daughter and back up. "If this ends up being serious, good luck."

"You, too." Tracy stood by her flatbed loaded to the gills with so many things. She wanted to tell the young mother to hurry. That she needed so much more than just formula and water. But what if it amounted to nothing?

She grabbed the handle and exhaled. All she could do was prepare for herself and her family. She couldn't make the whole town do the same.

As she pushed the flatbed toward the checkouts, Tracy looked around her. So many people just going about their business buying supplies for their bakeries and restaurants and entertaining their kids in the early afternoon. No one panicking. No one buying for the end of the world except her and a young mother who only thought of her baby and not herself.

She entered an empty checkout line and the cashier took her membership card with a smile. "Our credit card machine is down. I hope you brought your checkbook."

Tracy nodded. "I did."

"Good. Then let's get you checked out and on your way."

Tracy watched the cash register display as the cashier scanned in every item. She had never spent this much at a store before. The grocery store bill had been high, but this would wipe out her checking account.

She still needed to withdraw some cash and fill up her gas tank, too. Thankfully, she could write a check and transfer the difference over from savings before it cleared. She hated to dip into their emergency fund, but wasn't this exactly what it was for? Emergencies.

The cashier announced the total. "That'll be $1,311.62."

Tracy almost choked, but she managed to fill out the check and sign it without throwing up. Over a thousand dollars.

She took the receipt with shaky fingers and headed toward the exit. The man at the door took the receipt with a smile. "Stocking up?"

"Mm-hmm."

"Good for you. It's always good to have some extra on hand."

Tracy reclaimed the receipt and grunted as she got the flatbed started again. She pushed it to the Suburban and opened up the back.

She struggled to fit everything she bought along with the groceries from her trip to the supermarket, but Tracy managed somehow. As she slid into the driver's seat, her phone buzzed in her pocket.

Relief flooded her veins. The phones were working again. It had to be either her daughter or Walter. She pulled out the phone and frowned.

Emergency Presidential Alert.
Severe Space Weather Warning in this area until 08:00 AM PST.
Take Shelter Now. Dusk to Dawn Curfew in Effect.

What? Oh, no. Tracy's heart sank. *It's true.*

As she sat there in shock, another text came in. This time from her daughter.

I'm on the way home. Stay safe. I'll be there soon.

Tracy couldn't wait another second. She tossed her phone on the passenger seat and put the car in reverse. *I need to hurry.*

CHAPTER EIGHT

TRACY

Sacramento, CA
    5:30 p.m.

The highway hadn't moved a foot in more than twenty minutes. In the time it had taken Tracy to drive to the closest on-ramp and merge into traffic, everyone else in the entire city must have decided to do the same thing.

Cars and trucks and tractor trailers clogged all three lanes in both directions, bumpers almost touching. Hordes of people sat in their vehicles watching the afternoon sun set through grimy windows. Everyone was going nowhere fast.

It was a powder keg of inactivity. One spark, one raised voice or fender bump, and the whole place would blow. Tracy checked the locks on the Suburban for the hundredth time. The weight of the supplies behind her bore down on her mind like a pile of bricks, hard and unyielding.

If anyone saw what she had... If anyone tried to take it...

A commotion a few cars up snapped her out of her spiraling thoughts. A man slammed the door to his little hatchback and glowered at the pickup behind him. Shouts filtered through the pileup, but Tracy couldn't make out the words.

When the man in the truck stuck his hand out the window, the meaning of his gesture was plain even without the words to go with it. The guy standing in the road didn't appreciate it. He bellowed as he gesticulated, face coloring to match the setting sun.

Had the truck hit his car? Tracy couldn't believe it. Why did some people lose their cool in traffic? It's not like freaking out would get them anything.

A loud pop sounded and Tracy jumped in her seat, slamming her knee into the steering wheel. *What the...? It sounded like... It couldn't be.*

Tracy watched in growing disbelief as the door to the pickup truck opened, a puny squeak in comparison to the gunshot the man inside had fired up into the air. He held the handgun up high and pointed the barrel toward the sky. A warning shot.

As he clambered out of the truck, he changed position, aiming straight for Mr. Hatchback's chest. *Back down. Just back down.* She waited with bated breath. The man stood his ground, planting his feet a bit wider in the asphalt as he crossed his arms over his chest. *Oh, no.*

Tracy glanced in her rear view. She had a foot between her bumper and the car behind her. She checked the side of the road. A quarter-mile of dirt and weeds before the exit ramp opened up.

More shouts drew Tracy's attention back to the scene in front. A handful of people had gotten out of their cars and approached the two men. Were they there to talk the pair down or amp them up? Tracy never understood why people crowded around a fight to watch. Shouldn't they be trying to stop it?

Mr. Pickup fired the gun again, this time at Mr. Hatchback's feet. One of the onlookers jumped back. The bullet had ricocheted past him and into the side of the closest car. This was insane. Someone was going to get killed and what would happen then? A riot? Worse?

Sweat beaded at the edges of Tracy's hairline and her palms grew clammy. She couldn't wait another minute. Sitting there in traffic with a mountain of food and drinks and supplies made her a lucrative target. If a mob formed, she'd never survive.

With one hand on the gear shift, Tracy put the Suburban in reverse. She eased her foot off the brake, ready to inch backward when a tapping on her driver's side window made her jerk.

"Excuse me! Do you have any spare gas?" A woman stood too close to her window, peering into the back. Her hair was pulled back in a haphazard ponytail and the sallow, sunken pits of her cheeks spoke of years of drug or alcohol abuse. Maybe both.

The stranger pointed a dirt-caked finger at a rusted

a VW beetle with a cracked back window. "We're on fumes. Can you help us out?"

When did my throat get so dry? Tracy smacked her tongue against the roof of her mouth, trying to manufacture some spit. "I-I'm s-sorry. I don't have any gas."

"You got a whole lotta other shit, though, dontcha?" Tracy whipped her head around as a shiver of fear twitched her fingers.

A man stood on the other side of her car, face pressed to the glass, hands blocking out the sun so he could see inside. "Woo-wee. What's that, six cases of water?" He pulled back and shouted over the roof of the car. "You see that Becky? She's got enough food in there to feed this whole damn traffic jam."

The man swayed as he stood, the wispy bits of his dishwater hair falling in his face. He couldn't have weighed more than Tracy despite his height. He picked at a graying tooth as he motioned toward the back seat, a gaping hole in his mouth where a canine should be. "You wanna be nice and open up? We'll only take a little. Ain't that right, baby?"

When did the car get so hot? Tracy couldn't breathe. Her chest rose and fell but the air seared her lungs like smoke. How many people were on her already? How many were out there, listening to the pair of them rant about all her supposed riches? The back end of her SUV dipped and Tracy snapped her gaze to the rear view. A pair of dirty jeans was all she could see. Someone was standing on her rear bumper.

Oh my God.

She tried to swallow, but her sandpaper tongue scraped across the roof of her mouth. "G-Get off my car!"

"*Oooh.* She wants you to get down, Dwayne. Guess you better listen to the little lady."

The Suburban bobbed up and down. Dwayne was jumping.

Tracy glanced around her, squinting into the neighboring cars. Someone would help her, wouldn't they? They wouldn't just leave her like this.

A door to the car in front of her opened and Tracy sucked in a breath. *Thank you so much.* She smiled at the man as he turned to face her, but the corners of her mouth fell as he eyed her. There was no sympathy on his pinched face.

He pointed at the back of her SUV. "I've been out here two hours. I'm hot, my wife is thirsty. If you've got supplies. Let's see them."

No. Nonononono. This can't be happening.

It had only been a few hours. They were only stuck in traffic. *People shouldn't be doing this. It isn't right.*

"Please, just leave me alone." Tracy's gaze darted between Becky on her left, the boyfriend on the right, the new guy in front of her, and her rear view, where she could barely make out Dwayne as he tested the strength of her tow hitch.

They weren't going to leave her alone. Tracy inhaled, shoving a breath full of heat and courage down into her lungs. *Now or never.* She wasn't going to be a casualty of a traffic jam and fear. Not today.

She shifted the Suburban into reverse. The boyfriend's head snapped up and she focused on him, glowering in defiance as she punched the gas. The Suburban lurched backward and Dwayne cried out as he fell onto the hood of the car behind her.

Tracy didn't look and she didn't stop. She shoved the gear shift into drive and hit the accelerator again.

Everyone in front and beside her jumped back. Becky screamed something about Dwayne's leg, but Tracy tuned it out. She'd made her choice. Now all she could do was get the heck out of there and hope no one followed her.

The Suburban bounced over the rumble strip and fishtailed as she accelerated into the grass. In seconds it was over; the horror of the traffic jam nothing more than dust in her rear view. It wasn't enough. She wouldn't ever be far enough away. Tracy gripped the steering wheel until her knuckles turned white, holding onto the faded leather like it was her sanity.

Please let me make it off the highway. Please.

Bouncing and bumping down the shoulder, Tracy veered into the exit lane and off the ramp, finally braving a glance behind her. So far, no one was following her. But she couldn't let her guard down. They could still come for her. She had to put enough distance between her and the exit that no one could find her.

Ten minutes later, she finally took a deep breath. She cracked the window and fresh air hit her in the face. *I did it. I got away.*

She blinked her surroundings into focus. For the past

few minutes, all Tracy did was drive. She needed miles between her and the highway. With another breath, she slowed to a stop, peering up at the street signs above her as the light turned red.

Not having a typical nine-to-five job, Tracy never needed to use the back roads. The highway was never busy when she needed to cross town. She hadn't been in this area in years.

She tapped on the navigation system of the SUV and waited for it to place her car on the map. She tapped it again. Nothing happened.

Great.

Now she could add getting lost to the list of good ideas she'd had since leaving work that afternoon.

Think, Tracy, think. She needed to head west. She could do that. As long as she pointed her car at the afternoon sun, she'd make it to a road she recognized. Eventually.

After twenty minutes that felt like twenty years, the area began to look familiar. Tracy snorted as it dawned on her.

She was back where she started, only a few blocks from the library. She turned onto the main road, slowing down to drive by the closed library building when a figure standing at the bus stop caught her eye.

Is that? It can't be. She slowed further, creeping up to the woman as she rolled down the passenger window. "Wanda? Is that you?"

The head librarian squinted as she peered into the car. "Tracy? What are you doing here?"

"The highway's a mess. I ran to Costco and got stuck. How about you? I thought you'd have left hours ago."

Wanda pushed up her glasses. "I stayed a little late to tidy up. I was just leaving when that strange alert came in. Did you see it?"

Tracy nodded. "What about the bus?"

Wanda gave a faltering smile. "It hasn't shown up."

Tracy bit her lip and glanced at the back of her car. She couldn't leave Wanda there on the side of the road. She wasn't like those bullies on the highway. She was a good person. Tracy could trust her.

She smiled and unlocked the car. "How about you hop in? I don't think we can get across town to your place with the traffic and the curfew, but you're welcome to stay with me tonight. I can drive you home tomorrow."

Wanda opened her mouth, but shut it without saying a word. Her simple cotton dress blew in the breeze. After a moment of staring at her watch and then the empty street, she turned back to Tracy. "Why are you doing this?"

"What do you mean?"

"Helping me."

Tracy blinked. "Because it's the right thing to do."

Wanda pursed her lips. "All right. I'll come." She tugged open the door to Tracy's SUV and climbed inside, pausing as the back full of everything from protein bars to toilet paper came into view. "Wow. When you do Costco, you really do Costco."

Tracy let a laugh slip from her lips. "You know what the Girl Scouts say."

Wanda cocked her head. "No, what?"

"Be prepared." Tracy put the car in drive and pulled back onto the road. "Come on, let's go home."

This time, she hoped the drive would be uneventful, but with the Presidential Alert and the incident from the highway fresh in her mind, Tracy knew it couldn't be that easy.

She thought of her daughter and her text, *I'm coming.* A nugget of fear lodged itself in Tracy's heart.

CHAPTER NINE

MADISON

Yolo Causeway
   6:30 p.m.

"We haven't moved in three hours. I vote we ditch the car and walk."

Madison's head jerked up out of the half-doze she'd fallen into. They were still stuck on the causeway, the stretch of elevated highway between Davis and West Sacramento. It was the only direct way into Sacramento and the fastest way to reach Madison's house. Ordinarily, anyway.

She sat up in her seat and wiped at her eyes. "Tucker, you can't be serious. We're still thirty miles from my parents' house and over a hundred from Brianna's cabin. Her place is north of Truckee. You want to walk all that way?"

Tucker motioned at the windshield. "It beats this,

doesn't it?" He glanced at the clock and shook his head. "It's getting dark. The CME could be here soon. We need to get off the road and get somewhere safe."

"I thought you said eighteen hours."

He scratched his head. "It could be less. We don't really know."

Madison exhaled. "Try the radio again, Brianna."

Her roommate reached for the dial and turned it to the right. The same three beeps they had all heard since they could remember filled the car. "This is an alert. Severe weather may impact your area soon. Take shelter now. Dusk to dawn curfew in effect. This is an alert."

Brianna turned off the radio and pounded the steering wheel with her fists, blonde curls breaking free from her ponytail as she freaked out in the driver's seat. After a moment, she spoke, determination punching every word. "This is ridiculous. We need to get off the causeway, onto a side street, and make our way to Madison's place. We can sleep there tonight and hit the road first thing in the morning."

Peyton craned his neck to look at the sky. "We might not have the chance. Do you see that?"

"What?" Madison leaned over to find what Peyton pointed at. From her vantage point, it looked like the sunset was tinted green.

"Crap. We're too late."

Everyone in the car turned to Tucker. "What do you mean, too late?"

"What you're seeing? That's the northern lights."

"No way. We're way, way too far south."

"Not if the geomagnetic storm is here, we're not."

Brianna scrunched up her face, freckles disappearing in the creases. "It can't be here. We still have power. The car still works, so does my phone. An EMP could kill all that."

"Not a solar one. CMEs only cause E3 electromagnetic pulses. They don't knock out small electronics."

"Then what do they knock out?"

Tucker glanced up at the darkening sky before speaking. "The power grid."

"Oh, great. That's even better than a nuclear bomb. Our cars will work but no one will be able to pump gas or heat their homes or make any food. Awesome."

Peyton spoke up. "Everyone pack your bags. If we have to ditch the car at some point, we should be ready."

Madison opened her mouth to protest, but shut it just as quickly. She couldn't argue with Peyton's logic. He handed her the brand-new hiking pack she'd picked out and she twisted around to retrieve the rest of her gear.

Starting with the heaviest items first, Madison packed her bag. Water and food. Spare clothes and first aid supplies. Crank flashlight and a multi-tool. Hiking boots and a winter coat.

She cinched her sleeping bag down across the top and set the whole thing on the floorboard. If they had to bail, she'd be ready.

After everyone finished, Tucker broke the silence. "I still think we should go."

Brianna shook her head. "I'm not leaving the Jeep

unless we absolutely have to." She reached out and took his hand. "It's our ticket out of here, Tuck. If we leave it, how will we get to the cabin?"

A lock of hair fell across his eye and he pushed it back. "We'll walk."

"You really think we'll make it all that way on foot?"

Madison could hear the fear in Brianna's voice. It wasn't that she didn't trust her boyfriend, or believe him when he said they should walk. Brianna's father had taught her all about survival. She knew never to leave the safety of a vehicle if you didn't have to. Tucker hadn't grown up like Madison's roommate. He didn't share the same concerns.

"Brianna's right. We shouldn't leave the Jeep unless we don't have a choice. It's safer in here than it is out there. We don't have any weapons. We'll be carrying a ton of gear. It'll look like—"

Peyton spoke up. "We're easy targets."

Brianna shook her head. "Worse. We'll look like prey."

"Seriously?" Tucker rolled his eyes. "The four of us will be together. That'll scare anybody off."

Brianna disagreed. "No, it won't. As soon as people see what we have, they'll try to steal it. That's what people do."

"Tucker might be right, Brianna." Madison scooted forward in her seat. "We shouldn't think the worst of people already. None of us would ever attack someone just because they had something we needed."

Brianna twisted in the driver's seat to look Madison in the eye. "What if you were hungry? Thirsty? What if you realized this was the beginning of the end? I don't think any one of us knows what we'd do in that situation."

Madison scoffed. "Don't be ridiculous. You seriously think that I'd turn into some criminal just because the power went out?"

"Not at first. But other people won't hesitate. You think too much of your fellow man, Madison."

She'd heard similar sentiments before. When Madison tried to recruit other agricultural students to establish a homeless garden, only a handful of students offered to help. The rest begged off saying they were too busy or didn't think it would do any good.

A few told her that *those people* weren't worth helping. It would be throwing all that hard work away since the people they helped were drug addicts and ex-cons. It didn't make any sense to Madison. So they were down on their luck. So a few might have criminal pasts. It didn't mean they were beyond help.

Everyone needed assistance now and then.

Madison turned to look out the window. A series of telephone poles with wires strung between them stood just beyond the edge of the causeway. She squinted to get a closer look.

Are those sparks?

"Uh… guys…"

Brianna wasn't paying attention. She was too busy spouting off reasons Madison was the resident Pollyanna to listen.

The sparks grew, showers of orange and yellow falling into the basin below. "You really should look…"

Tucker talked over her, offering his own reasons for humanity to fall into the gutter when Madison shouted. "Guys! Over there!"

She pointed out the window where the power lines were now hissing and sputtering with current.

"Shit." Tucker's one curse said it all.

Brianna turned to her boyfriend. "What is it?"

He pointed at the sparks. All four of them watched as the sparks ran along the lines and hit a small transformer attached to one of the telephone poles. It exploded, sending a burst of smoke into the air and a shower of sparks down all around it.

Another transformer about ten poles away followed. Then another. And another.

All the way down the causeway, the electrical lines popped and hissed, transformers overloading and catching fire one after the next.

"That," Tucker said, pointing at the devastation, "is what happens with an E3 EMP. It's here."

"Oh my God." Madison brought her hand up to her lips as she looked out into the night. The lights that had begun to glow in front of them, signaling the end of the causeway and the start of city, blinked out in a wave. Whole sections of West Sacramento went dark before her eyes.

She turned around to look out the back window, but she couldn't see anything but the headlights of the cars behind them. The buildings she knew were only a mile away stood dark.

The lights were out. The grid was gone.

"Do you really think…" She trailed off, unsure of what to even ask.

Peyton pulled out his cell phone. "No service. The cell towers must be down."

Madison swiped her phone on. *Zero bars.* She dialed 911, the one number that was supposed to work no matter what. Not even a dial tone. Nothing.

She swallowed down the rising wave of panic in her throat. The magnitude of it began to hit her. No power meant no emergency services, and 911 wouldn't know where to send anyone without GPS. Without the phones, they wouldn't receive any calls.

Cars would work, but for how long? What about hospitals? Prisons? If they were dark, what would happen to all the people clinging to life and the criminals that society had deemed too dangerous to be on the streets?

Tucker and Brianna were right. Peyton, too. She'd completely underestimated this thing. They weren't prepared at all.

How would she ever make it to her mom? She didn't even know where her dad was right then. Had he flown to Hong Kong? Did his flight get canceled? He could be flying over the North Pole right now, sitting on the tarmac at the airport, or be oblivious to all of this halfway around the world.

How would he make it home?

She glanced up at the front seat where Brianna and Tucker stared out the windows, eyes wide. How would Brianna find her parents? Were they up at the cabin or stuck on the road just like them?

No one was ready. No one could handle something like this. Madison looked around her at all the cars on the causeway. A man next to them had gotten out of his Prius and stood next to it, staring at the closest burning telephone pole.

What would any of these people do now?

She reached for Peyton's hand and squeezed. At least they had each other. Together they would survive. They would make it to her house and regroup, no matter how long it took. They had to.

CHAPTER TEN

MADISON

Yolo Causeway

7:30 p.m.

"You're sure?"

Brianna nodded. "I don't see any other way. No one is moving. People are out of their cars, milling around. It's going to get ugly soon. We need to leave."

She rubbed her hand across the leopard-print cover to her steering wheel. "It's a damn shame. I love this car."

"We can come back for it." Madison knew it wasn't true, but she offered it anyway. "When everything calms down, we can come get it."

"No. We can't." Brianna glanced up, her eyes glassy with tears. "Don't you get it? Nothing's ever going to calm down. Nothing's ever going to be the same again."

Madison couldn't believe her friend who'd planned for something like this her whole life was the one freaking out. Brianna's family had prepped for everything from a natural disaster to an all-out nuclear war. If anyone could handle a geomagnetic storm, it was Brianna.

With a smile Madison hoped looked convincing, she reached out and patted her roommate's hand. "Don't say that. We'll be okay. We're together. That has to count for something."

"Hey, guys?" Tucker's voice edged with alarm. "I hate to interrupt this Hallmark moment and all, but I think we've got a problem." He leaned forward in his seat, peering into the dusk.

"What is it?"

The semi one lane over rumbled to life, vibrating the backseat.

"I think the trucker is sick of waiting."

"But he's trapped." Madison squinted, pressing her hands to the glass of the door window. As far as she could see, cars stacked up like dominos, every lane worse than the next. The tractor trailer sat sandwiched between the guardrail on one side and cars in front, back, and on the other side. "He can't go anywhere."

The blare of the truck's horn made Madison jump. She banged her knee on Tucker's seat back and winced. "What is he doing?"

"Making room."

What? It didn't make sense. He might have a bigger vehicle, but they were stuck on a bridge over the Yolo Bypass floodplain. Cars couldn't move off to the shoulder to make room; they would fall off straight off the side.

The horn blared again. Madison swallowed, the back of her throat tightening as she stared out the window.

A figure rushed past Madison's window, running between the cars. More blur than man, Madison only caught a glimpse of his beard and red baseball cap before he disappeared in front of the truck. She hissed out a question. "What's he doing?"

"Causing a scene, I think."

Brianna cracked her window and tense shouts filtered into the back seat.

"—can't just—"

"—don't care if—"

Madison strained to listen, concentrating on the fleeting bits of argument she could make out over the steady roar of the massive engine.

"—out of the way, then—"

"—nna kill somebo—"

The truck lurched, bouncing forward as the driver shifted gears and eased off the brake. The whole causeway trembled.

Madison's chest constricted, lungs tight with held breath. "He can't be serious."

"Oh, he's serious all right." Brianna grabbed her keys and shoved them in the ignition. "Everybody buckle up. This might be our chance."

"What? No!" Madison reached out, clawing into the back of Tucker's seat. The fabric dented beneath her fingernails as she dug for purchase. The trucker was just showing off. He had to be.

Madison ground her teeth back and forth, forcing the rising panic in her chest down.

A man shouted, arms waving as he ran toward the cars in front of them. He was warning them. Madison reached for the door handle and yanked. The door wouldn't open.

"Let me out!"

"So you can get yourself killed? No way."

Madison jiggled the handle. Nothing. "Unlock the door, Brianna. Someone needs to warn those people."

"It isn't going to be you." Her roommate turned around in the front seat, brown eyes narrowed straight on Madison. "Sit down."

"No!" Madison scrabbled at the door lock, digging her nails into the crevice it disappeared into, trying to unlock the car.

Brianna turned back to the front and started the engine. "If you get out of this car, I'm leaving you behind."

"What are you talking about? We're stuck on the bridge!" Madison yanked the door handle again before banging into the molded plastic with her shoulder. It had to give. She had to warn those people.

The truck driver laid on the horn. Madison jerked up, staring out the window in disbelief. He was going to do it. He was actually going to mow those cars in front of him down. "We have to help them."

Peyton's hand wrapped around her wrist and he pulled her away from the door. "We can't, Madison."

"Yes, we can. We can yell, shout… anything."

"And then what? Get run over by all the cars behind us?"

"They wouldn't do that."

Peyton's lips thinned into a line. "If you really think that, then you haven't been around desperate people." He let go of her wrist. "You need to think about yourself first. Or your family, Madison. Not these strangers."

The truck driver hit the horn again, but this time he didn't let up. It kept on sounding, a tortured wail of last warning as he hit the gas. At first, the cab moved like a giant, slow and ungainly, with stops and starts.

But the harder the driver punched the gas, the more the lumbering beast accelerated. A handful of people Madison hadn't even seen jumped back from the cab of the truck, shouting and shaking their fists.

She watched, eyes wide in horror, as the truck hit the first car in front of it. A little white hatchback of a thing, it never stood a chance.

Metal crunched and groaned and tore, the sickening sounds of anger and impatience cutting through the silence of the near-dark.

Madison's hand flew to her mouth as Brianna shifted the Jeep into drive.

"Everybody hold on. This is gonna get nasty." Brianna gripped the steering wheel, primed and ready.

All Madison could do was watch. The hammering of her heart eclipsed the sounds of destruction and the shouts of other motorists. It even drowned out the rush of her breath sawing in and out of her lungs like she'd run a marathon.

The truck moved again, lurching forward as it shoved the little white economy car out the way. Brianna seized the opportunity, leaping into the gap left between the back end of the trailer and the car behind it.

Taking advantage of a madman's decision wasn't how this should go. She should be out there, helping the people displaced by the truck, warning others to get to safety. Instead, Madison sat in the backseat like a fugitive on the run, hunched down for protection as Brianna tore through the gap left in the trailer's wake.

Every car length, the truck picked up speed, smashing into the next vehicle with more force, hitting the next with more acceleration. They flew behind it, safe in the space right up against the trailer's bumper, avoiding the smashed cars shoved into the concrete railing on one side and into each other on the other.

They followed the wake of destruction, riding it out like a water skier behind a jet boat. Only instead of the ocean and sunshine, wrecked cars and screaming people greeted them with every wave.

Madison closed her eyes. She couldn't watch. She couldn't bear witness to the heartless actions of the truck driver another second.

After what seemed like an eternity, Brianna whooped from the front seat. "We did it!"

A hand landed on Madison's back, rubbing up and down until she sat up and opened her eyes. They were off the causeway. Off the highway entirely, cruising down a quiet side street in the dark, their headlights the only illumination as far as Madison could see.

Madison blinked and looked around, the tightness in her chest finally receding. "We made it?"

Brianna glanced up at her in the rear view. "Still think we should have stayed behind?"

She exhaled. *Yes. No.* Madison didn't know anymore. If they had stayed on the causeway helping other motorists, would they have made it off the bridge without incident? What if someone found out what they had in the back of the Jeep? She glanced down at the stuffed backpack on the floor in front of her.

Brianna had a point, but surely humanity still meant something. People didn't turn into animals the second disaster struck.

At least not everyone.

She glanced out at the darkness, unease creeping into the gaping wound the events of the bridge had opened in her mind. "I don't think we should be driving in the dark."

"Why not? We want to get to your mom's, don't we?"

"Yeah, but haven't you noticed? We're the only lights out here. What if someone sees us or tries to stop us? I don't even know where we are."

"It's not totally dark." Brianna glanced up out the windshield at the arcing colors in the sky. "People won't notice us."

Peyton spoke up. "Madison has a point. We should conserve our fuel. Park somewhere, get some sleep. Drive when it's light out."

Tucker pointed out the window. "Looks like a park up ahead. We could pull off, maybe drive into those trees. No one would see us out there if we kill the lights."

Brianna shut them off and the road descended into darkness.

She idled for a moment on the asphalt, waiting until her eyes adjusted to the night. "All right. We'll park. Get some sleep. But we're taking shifts. Someone has to keep watch."

She drove slowly, peering into the darkness as she maneuvered around a stand of bushes and over the curb. With a few careful turns, Brianna hid the Jeep from the road behind a thicket of bushes and trees. No one could see them, even with the added light from the sky.

Peyton snorted as Brianna turned off the engine.

"What's so funny?"

"It reminds me of a B-horror movie setup. Teenagers going into the dark woods to escape the monster of the week."

Tucker lowered his seat. "Guess there won't be any more of those for a while, will there?"

Brianna shook her head. "Nope. Hell, they might never come back."

Madison frowned. None of this seemed real. She glanced around at her friends as they made themselves comfortable in their seats. No way could she sleep. Not after the incident on the bridge. She exhaled. "You all get some sleep. I'll take first watch."

CHAPTER ELEVEN

TRACY

Sacramento, CA
6:30 p.m.

"You sure you don't mind me staying the night? The bus depot isn't that far from here. You could drop me there, instead. I'm sure there's just a problem with the bus for my route. Another has to be coming."

Wanda tucked her hands in her lap, smiling at Tracy. Apart from superficial talk about Tracy's daughter in college and Wanda's recommendations for summer reading, they didn't know a lot about each other.

Tracy smiled back. "It's not a bother, really. Walt's not home, Madison's at school. It'll be nice to have someone to share the house with for a night." That wasn't the whole truth, but Wanda didn't seem to have a grip on the impending solar storm. Truth was, Tracy didn't think Wanda should be alone, and two heads had to be better than one, right?

"Thank you." Wanda went back to looking out the passenger window and fidgeting.

"Do you…" Tracy didn't want to pry, but if Wanda had someone waiting at home for her…

"It's just me right now. My cat passed away a few months ago and I haven't had the heart to get another one just yet."

Tracy exhaled, relieved to not have to drive across town tonight. They could stay on the smaller roads, head straight to Tracy's house, and make it home before anything bad happened.

The traffic light in front of them turned yellow and Tracy slowed, pulling up to a stop behind a small four-door sedan as the light changed to red.

Wanda pointed out the front window, pushing her glasses up her nose as she squinted. "Is the light flickering or is it just me?"

Tracy glanced up at the traffic light. The red light didn't flicker… It pulsed, growing brighter then fading again and again.

Like it was charged with too much current.

Oh no. Nononono. Tracy looked out the window at the lines of telephone poles stretching down the street. The neighborhood they were driving through was built in the fifties. Tiny little ranches and bungalows all in a line with power lines stretched across telephone poles and into the houses. Just like Tracy's own neighborhood built a decade before.

There were more wires hanging from the telephone

poles than leaves on the walnut tree in the yard next door. Tracy watched, breath caught in her lungs. Was this it? Was it really happening?

The light in front of them turned green and the sedan one car ahead began to move when the entire traffic light exploded. Bits of metal and plastic flew in all directions and the wires connecting the light to the poles arced in the air.

A hissing, sputtering sound grew louder and louder and the transformer perched on the telephone pole closest to Tracy's SUV burst into flames. Electrical wires snapped in half, their live ends flailing about as the whole power grid flooded with current.

It was just like Joe described, but way, way too early. The CME had arrived.

Tracy scanned the neighborhood, watching in shock as house after house snapped to black. The street lights rolled out in a wave, the traffic lights blinked out, and in a matter of seconds, power to the entire area shut off.

Oh my God. Tracy's hand flew to her mouth. *It's real.* Everything Joe warned her about had actually happened. Tracy's thoughts flew to her daughter and her husband. Where were they? What were they doing? Madison's last text put a whole new sense of urgency into Tracy. Her daughter was out there somewhere, trying to make it home.

She didn't know if she was safe or in danger or possibly worse. *I have to protect her.*

Wanda shrieked beside her and Tracy almost jumped out of her seat. In her own panic, she'd forgotten the woman was even there.

"The telephone pole is on fire! And that one is too!" Wanda pointed farther down the street, her painted red nail directed at another fire about twenty yards away. "What is going on?"

Tracy swallowed. "Didn't you see the Presidential Alert?"

"What are you talking about?"

"On your phone. Didn't you get an alert?"

Wanda reached down between her feet and pulled up a zebra-print handbag. She fished out a little brick of a phone and powered it on. "I don't turn my phone on during work hours." She cast a sideways glance at Tracy. "It *is* the library."

Tracy couldn't have stared any harder. *She doesn't know?* All the time they were driving, all the time Wanda had been standing at the bus stop, holding her purse and hoping for the bus…

Wanda didn't know the whole world was about to change?

A shout from outside made them both look up. The sedan in front of them sat in the middle of the intersection, a wire draped across its roof. The couple inside were twisting about, looking out the windows and waving.

"What's going on?" Wanda's voice edged higher than its normal bubbly soprano.

A man on the street corner shouted again. "I can't get through to 911!" He waved his arms at the couple in the car, but they weren't paying attention.

Tracy looked at the wire, tracing it back to the

telephone pole still on fire at the street corner. All at once it made sense. She laid on the horn until the woman in the car glanced up.

"Don't get out." Tracy made a motion with her hands to curl up in a ball, shrugging her shoulders and holding them tight. "The wire! It could be hot!" She pointed at the wire draped across their car.

The woman shook her head and grabbed her husband by the shoulder. He turned to face Tracy.

She tried again. "The wire!" She gesticulated, jabbing her index finger in the air toward the pole. "It could still have a charge. Stay inside the car!"

Wanda shook her head. "They should get out. Won't they get electrocuted in there?"

"No. As long as they stay in the car and don't touch any of the metal, they'll be fine. It's when they try to get out that they'll get hurt."

Tracy rolled down her window and cupped her hands to her mouth. "Don't touch anything metal!"

The man on the corner stepped off the sidewalk and headed toward the car. Tracy tried to wave him off. "Don't! You'll get hurt!"

He stopped in the middle of the road. "They need help."

"You'll get electrocuted."

"Are you sure?" Wanda peered out through the windshield, never once moving from her seat. "What if the car catches on fire?"

Tracy glanced over at her. "Then they'll have to jump free. But until then, they should stay put. If the metal parts of the car have been charged, just touching it will be enough."

Wanda scoffed. "You can't expect them to just sit in there forever. They want to get home just like everyone else stuck here." She waved around at the man in the street and the other cars facing them across the road.

"The car in front of us won't go anywhere if that couple is dead." Tracy turned back to the sedan just as the bystander reached the car. Tracy shoved her door open, standing up to yell. "No! Stay back!"

He paused, hand outstretched for the car. But it was too late. The woman inside reached for the door handle on her own. One touch of the metal handle and she jerked like a marionette on a string, flying backward and into her husband's arms. He grabbed her, wrapping his arms around her as he turned to open his own door.

"No!" Tracy shouted again, but it all happened too fast. The bystander rushed in, waving his arms and yelling, but the passenger didn't stand a chance.

Just as his wife had been electrocuted, so too, was he. His body jumped and twitched in the seat as the current passed through him. In moments it was over.

He slumped over in the front seat, torso draped over the body of his wife. Nothing but the tops of their heads and wisps of smoke were visible.

Tracy lowered herself back into her car and shut the door.

"A-are… t-they…?" Wanda couldn't finish the question.

Tracy nodded. "I think so."

"Wow. I guess you were right."

Tracy cut Wanda a glance as she put the Suburban in reverse. She backed up until she was a safe distance away and turned around.

The man from the sidewalk still stood in the road, useless cell phone in his hand, staring in shock.

"Shouldn't you go help them?"

Tracy put the SUV in drive and headed back the way they had come. "I tried. They didn't listen. There's nothing anyone can do for them now."

"What about the police? Shouldn't someone call?"

A million responses came to mind, but Tracy shoved them all down. She turned the corner onto another street without power and shrugged. "Knock yourself out. My guess is you won't have much luck."

Wanda turned on her phone and tinkered with it while Tracy tried to make sense of all that just happened. Every street she turned down looked the same. No lights. No sound.

Nothing but the rumble of the Suburban's engine and its headlights as she navigated by memory home. The CME must have caused the EMP Joe warned about, frying the circuits and the transformers from here to the East Coast, if not more.

Maybe it was just a local outage, but Tracy didn't think so. In the morning she could attempt to find out. Drive around, see what might not be impacted. But for now, they needed to get somewhere safe. Secure.

Wanda jabbed at her phone's screen, red nail clicking with every poke. "Silly thing. It's not connecting to anything. Says I have no service." She frowned and glanced out the window. "I always have service here."

Tracy didn't have it in her to break the news to Wanda that night. Let the woman have one more good night's sleep before she learned the world she knew and took for granted was gone.

If it really was true.

She turned down her own street and exhaled, hoping beyond hope that the rest of the country was blissfully unaware of the power outage here in Sacramento. *Please let it be local. Small and manageable.*

If the whole country were hit… Tracy didn't know how long anyone would survive.

She pulled into her driveway and put the SUV in park before hopping out. "I'll be right back." Jogging up to her dark front step, she unlocked the door, rushed though the house and entered the garage. From there, she disengaged the power garage opener and pulled up the garage door by hand.

As she hopped back into the driver's seat Wanda glanced over at her. "Do you have a microwave? I sure could do with a warm glass of milk."

Tracy pulled into the garage and put the car in park before resting her head on the steering wheel. Explaining the future to Wanda wasn't going to be easy.

DAY TWO

CHAPTER TWELVE

TRACY

Sacramento, CA
    7:30 a.m.

Coffee. Hot, steaming coffee made from fresh ground beans that cost more per pound than organic, free-range, patted and petted and called-by-name chickens from the fancy market one neighborhood over.

It was the one thing above everything else Tracy would miss. She loved coffee. Sure, she would get used to the freeze-dried stuff mixed in a tepid cup of water, if she even had any water to spare, but darn.

Good coffee could turn a whole day around.

She tucked a leg up under her and looked over the list again. After she'd gotten Wanda tucked away in the guest bedroom with a portable lantern and shown her the shelf of books above the dresser, Tracy had unloaded the Suburban.

Cases of water and Gatorade. Giant packs of toilet paper and paper towels. Boxes of granola bars and big plastic tubs of protein powder. It all went into stacks along the wall of her bedroom. She'd done well, but no matter how much she stocked up, it would all run out.

And that was if no one found out she had it. She glanced down at the list. Everything she had in the kitchen. The food in the fridge. The extra supplies sequestered in her bedroom. All spelled out.

She could make it last.

The door to the guest bedroom squeezed open and a sleepy Wanda padded into the kitchen, wearing the same dress as the day before. Instead of her usual bun, Wanda's hair trailed down her back in a loose braid, a few gray strands hanging free around her face.

"Did you sleep well?"

"I did. It's amazing how well you can sleep when there's no noise. At my apartment, there's always cars buzzing by, or the bus picking up, or people out late and talking on the street. You live in such a quiet neighborhood."

Tracy leaned back in her chair. "It's not the neighborhood. It's the lack of electricity."

Wanda perked up. "It still hasn't come back on?"

"No. And I don't think it will. Not for a long time."

"What do you mean?"

Tracy motioned toward the chair. "You should sit down. I can't make coffee, but I can get you a glass of water if you'd like. I have some apple juice we should drink in the fridge too, since it's been opened."

"Water would be great."

Tracy stood up before pulling a glass from the cabinet above the sink. She filled it with a pitcher standing on the counter.

"What's with all the water?" Wanda pointed at all the containers lining the counter. Every possible pitcher, vase, or decently sized Tupperware Tracy owned sat on the counter, full of water.

"If it's bad as I think it is, the water will run out very soon. We need to save as much as we can."

Wanda frowned and took the glass from Tracy. "I don't understand. Isn't it just a power outage?"

Tracy exhaled and lowered herself back into her chair. *Now or never.* "The Presidential Alert that went out yesterday warned of severe space weather. Told everyone to shelter in place."

"Space weather?"

"Mm-hmm."

"I was an English major in college, Tracy. Not a scientist."

Tracy exhaled. "Then I'll start at the beginning. Stop me with questions."

Half an hour later, Tracy and Wanda polished off a breakfast of yogurt and chopped fruit that wouldn't last the day without power. But food only satisfied physical hunger, not concussion and curiosity.

Wanda ran her fingers up and down the near-empty water glass, brows knit in thought. "So you're saying a giant electromagnetic pulse knocked out the power to possibly the entire country?"

Tracy held up her hands. "I don't really know. It could be everywhere."

Wanda shook her head, her lips opening and closing as she tried to process everything Tracy had said. "But surely the government has prepared for something like this. The military will come. Or the National Guard. Or FEMA. Someone will be here to help us, won't they?"

"Maybe. After a while." Tracy sipped her own water and glanced out the window to the street. The first rays of morning sun hit her front porch and a little wren landed on the railing. Did the animals notice the difference? The lack of electricity? Or was it just another beautiful day to them?

She turned back to Wanda. "Without power, how can they communicate?"

"Your car didn't stop working. My cell phone still turns on. We're not totally without power."

"But the grid is down. When the battery runs out in your phone, how will you charge it?"

Wanda glanced down at her lap. "I don't know."

"What about the gas pumps? Without electricity, who will keep the gas flowing?"

"Some gas stations have backup power. Generators, that sort of thing."

"Those will work for a while. But when they run out of fuel, then what? Think about it. There won't be any electricity for grocery stores or hospitals. Police stations or prisons."

Wanda's eyes went wide.

"How long do you think the government can keep the peace if the very people who we rely on to protect us have their own families to think about?"

"You mean the police?"

Tracy nodded. "And the military and firefighters and EMTs. Everyone we rely on to keep us safe. They have families. Some of whom might not have any food in their house or water sitting on their counter."

Wanda chewed on her lower lip, the tell of insecurity softening the wrinkles around her mouth. "I don't think you're giving the government enough credit. People won't just abandon their posts. They'll do their jobs. It might take a little while, but we'll be fine."

"Are you going to the library this morning?"

Wanda blinked. "The… the power's out! How could I even open?"

Tracy shrugged. "Don't you think other people are going to think the same thing?"

Wanda might not want to admit it, but police officers and firefighters and members of the military were just like them. Scared and confused and unsure what to do next.

If they were faced with making sure their family had food, shelter, and water to survive versus going to work and helping strangers, Tracy didn't think it would be a hard choice. She knew Walt was doing everything he could to get home this very minute. Assuming he was all right.

She pushed the worry aside. Her husband was a strong, dependable man. If he could get back to her, he would. Now Madison on the other hand…

Tracy twisted her cup of water around on the table. At nineteen years old Madison didn't have the life experience of her father. She didn't know how to handle a disaster like this. Was she really on her way home? Had she changed her mind and stayed on campus?

How long before life at the university fell apart?

Thinking about her daughter was why she'd been up to watch the sunrise and why she'd been out on the roads to run into Wanda at all. She glanced up at the woman she barely knew.

Wanda had to be in her mid-fifties, about ten years older than Tracy, if she had to guess. But instead of staying in shape and active like Tracy made a point of being, Wanda had let herself go. Tracy wouldn't get much help in the manual labor or self-defense department from Wanda, but maybe she had some other skills.

She smiled, hoping for the best. "I've inventoried the fridge and freezer. We have about a day or two before most everything goes bad. Mind helping me cook up the frozen meat? I've got a grill in the backyard and a smoker. We can use both to preserve at least some of it before we need to throw it away."

Wanda cast a wary glance at the fridge. "I'm not much of a cook."

Great. "It's a good time to learn."

The older woman's brows knit even tighter. "I was hoping you could take me to my place today. I need to change clothes. Shower."

Tracy sat still, forcing her face to not give away her internal shock. Did the woman not listen to anything she'd said this morning? She wouldn't be able to take a shower. At least not a hot one.

The city water supply might still be operational, but

how long would that last? They had to be running the filtration system on backup generators. Those wouldn't last more than a day. Nothing was hooked up to solar power or wind turbines here.

Some of the small towns to the west between Sacramento and the Bay may still be up and running. If they shut down their systems before the EMP hit, the wind turbines might still function.

If Tracy had outfitted the roof with solar panels, they might have survived. But she hadn't. Wanda's apartment certainly hadn't invested in any green energy, either. By the time she drove her home, any water still running would be ice cold and possibly not even clean.

But if that's what the woman wanted…

Tracy could have used the extra pair of hands. But an unwilling pair might be worse than none at all. She puffed out a breath of air and glanced out the side window to the street beyond.

Leaving her house with all the supplies inside wasn't ideal, but she would have to sooner or later. And she could fill up on gas before the local stations ran out of backup power. She knew the closest Shell had a generator: when the creek flooded and the power had been out for days, it was the only place still open.

Maybe she could even check out the neighborhood and assess who could be an ally and who to watch out for. Tracy stood up. "Okay. I'll take you home. But not one word to anyone about my supplies. Understood?"

Wanda tilted her head. "Okay. Sure. If that's what you want."

"It is." Tracy finished her water and set the empty

glass in the sink. "Give me a few minutes and I'll be ready."

Wanda smiled. "Thanks."

"Don't thank me until we get there." Tracy wasn't sure they'd even make it down the street.

CHAPTER THIRTEEN

MADISON

Sacramento, CA
5:00 a.m.

The pounding wouldn't quit. All those little hammers, jabbing away at her skull. Little pointed pick axes held by Snow White's dwarves, searching for diamonds.

She begged them to stop. "Please, I'm not a diamond mine."

But they only intensified their efforts, hammers becoming the beaks of a thousand woodpeckers, every one insistent on reaching her brain. They were starving and she was dinner.

Madison swiped at her head, trying to shoo them away. *Go. Get out of here you nasty birds. Why won't you listen?*

"I said open up!"

The banging intensified. Madison swore one of the birds opened its beak and spoke. *What the…?*

"Shit."

Brianna? What are you doing here? Consciousness threatened, but Madison liked the safety of the dark.

Someone shook her, tearing away the mask of sleep as a bright light hit her eyes. "Wake up. It's the cops."

Madison pried an eye open. *The cops?* She sat up, wincing as she moved her neck. Slumping over in the back seat of a Wrangler might not have been the best choice in beds. Rubbing at her stiff muscles, she blinked, bringing the interior of the Jeep into focus.

The light flashed in her eyes again and Madison's brain finally kicked into gear. A police officer stood outside the Jeep, one hand on his hip, one holding a flashlight bright enough to illuminate the bottom of the ocean.

"What's going on?"

Brianna pushed her hair off her face and reached for window controls. "Someone fell asleep on his shift." She eyed Peyton in the rear view and he winced like she'd slapped him.

"Sorry. I was tired."

Madison frowned. "Not as tired as me. What time is it?"

Tucker volunteered through a yawn. "Just after four in the morning."

Madison groaned. "I only slept for three hours. No wonder."

Brianna pushed the window button down and

plastered a friendly smile on her face. "Can I help you, officer?"

"ID and registration, please."

She nodded. "My ID is in my back pocket and my registration is in the glove box. I'll get them."

He waited, eyes intermittently darting up to monitor Madison and both guys. She didn't understand why he'd be interested in a Jeep parked off the road on a day like today. Didn't he have to deal with looting and riots already?

After fishing out the requested documentation, Brianna handed them over. "Is there a problem?"

He pulled the light down to read and Madison finally got a look at his face. He couldn't have been much older than them. Maybe a year or two on the force. New recruits always got the worst shifts.

He shoved her ID and registration back through the window and raised the flashlight to blind them all once again. "Everyone else. Hand over your identification."

Madison dug her wallet out of the backpack at her feet and both Peyton and Tucker lifted off the seats to get at their wallets. After they handed the cards up to Brianna, she held them out the window.

"We were just getting a little bit of sleep after getting stuck in traffic."

He scoured the IDs, holding each one up as he shined the flashlight first at Tucker, then Peyton, and finally Madison. At last, he handed them back. "Do you know it's illegal to park here after dark?"

"No." Brianna shook her head, blonde curls

bouncing as she glanced back at Madison. "I don't think any of us knew that."

Madison agreed. "We never meant to break the law. If we knew, we'd have parked somewhere else."

The police officer stepped back, inspecting the outside of the Jeep. "Why are you up here in the bushes? Do you have something to hide?"

Brianna shook her head even harder. "Not at all. We just wanted to be off the road. Get somewhere quiet, you know? After driving for hours, we were exhausted. Just looking to sleep."

He flashed his light into the backseat, lingering on Madison's overstuffed backpack. "What's in the pack?"

She hesitated. "Camping gear. We're on a road trip. Spring break hiking trip." She hoped her voice came across more convincing than it sounded in her head. Why was she so nervous? They didn't have anything to hide.

Not unless the cop wanted what they had.

He flashed his light over to Peyton. "Where are you headed?"

"Uhh…" Peyton glanced at Madison, panic in his eyes.

Crap. He didn't know the first thing about camping spots in Northern California. The boy had been raised in Los Angeles. He was lucky to know Sacramento was even part of the same state.

Tucker volunteered. "Redwood National Park. After we stop at Madison's mom's house. She's in Sacramento."

Madison nodded. "Carmichael, actually."

The cop didn't look amused. He motioned with the flashlight and Madison's stomach flipped over. "Everyone out."

"What for?" Brianna sat straighter in her seat, eyes trained on the police officer.

"Suspicion of illegal substances. I'm doing a sobriety check."

"No. You don't have probable cause."

Madison almost choked on her own spit. *What is Brianna doing? She'll get us arrested!* Madison glanced at Peyton, but he looked just as shocked as she felt.

The police officer raised his voice. "Out of the car. Now."

Madison started to move, but Brianna held up a hand. "Not until you tell me what probable cause you have to suspect either inebriation or the existence of alcohol or illegal substances in my vehicle. Until then, you can't ask us to get out."

Oh my gosh. Madison tried not to hyperventilate, breathing through her nose and out her mouth as she counted to ten and back to one. Now wasn't the time to get into a fight with a cop or make a stand on principle. They needed to get to her mom's place before anything else happened.

The cop took a step back. "I'm going to count to three and you are going to open that car door."

"And if I don't?"

He unholstered the firearm at his side and pulled it out, pointing both it and the flashlight right at Brianna's face. "Then I'll arrest you for disobeying a police officer and you can explain it to your parents when they come to jail to bail you out."

"Brianna!" Madison hissed at her roommate from the back seat. "Just get out and be nice. We don't have anything to hide!"

Brianna smiled at the police officer, but answered Madison through her teeth. "He doesn't have a right to search us or make us take a test. I know the law!"

"But we need to get home! We don't even know where we are!"

The police officer's voice rang out. "One!"

"Brianna, come on." Peyton scooted forward in his seat until he could touch Brianna on the shoulder. "We need to do what he says."

"Two!"

Madison swallowed down her panic and the bile that crept up her throat. This couldn't be happening.

"We're getting out. Hold on!" Tucker threw open the passenger-side door and unlocked the back seat doors at the same time.

"Tucker!"

"Sorry, babe. I don't want to get shot tonight." He held up his hands as he stood up.

Brianna rolled her eyes and shoved her door open. "Fine. But I'm telling you, I'm right about this."

The second her feet touched the ground, the cop grabbed her by the wrist and spun her around, slamming Brianna into the hood of her Jeep before grabbing her head and shoving it down.

"Hey! Watch it!"

He didn't even look up. "Be quiet if you don't want to end up in the back of my patrol car."

Brianna almost spat. "It can't fit all of us. You'll have to let someone go."

"I can call for backup."

"Oh, really? Does your radio even work?"

"Of course it works."

"Tried it lately?"

The cop hesitated. "No, actually. I haven't."

"Heard any chatter for a while?"

He glanced back toward the parking lot. "No."

"Unusual, isn't it? Haven't you stopped to wonder why the power is out all over?"

Brianna was getting to him. Every question she asked, he loosened his grip on her head. "It's just a blackout. That's why I'm on patrol. Every time the power goes out this neighborhood goes to shit."

"Oh, great. And this is where we decide to park." Peyton shook his head, his hands still raised in the air.

Tucker spoke up next. "You really don't know what's happened, do you?"

The cop blew him off. "I don't need to know. I just need to do my job. Hands on the hood, right where I can see them." He motioned with his pistol and Tucker complied, stepping up and palming the yellow metal.

"I really think you should let us go. If we're right about what happened last night, this part of town is going up like a tinderbox." Brianna angled to look the cop in the eye. "You should go home. Protect your family."

Madison took a step closer, hands raised. "The

power isn't ever coming back on. We were hit with a solar EMP. The grid is toast."

"You're making that up. That's some college speak you're just using to get me to let you go. You've probably got a bunch of weed in that backpack you don't want me to find."

Madison shook her head. "I don't use drugs or drink. Neither do my friends. Haven't you noticed the sky?"

The cop glanced up at the streaks of color.

"The northern lights prove it."

"You're bullshitting me.

Madison shook her head again. "We're not the people you should be worried about."

"Oh, yeah?" The cop almost smirked. "Who should I be worried about?"

"Yo!" A voice called out from behind the Jeep. "You should be worried about us, bro!"

CHAPTER FOURTEEN

MADISON

West Sacramento, CA
5:45 a.m.

The cop raised his gun, flashlight sweeping the area behind the vehicle where the voice came from. Madison froze, too afraid to turn around. She knew this area was home to more gang members than others, but when they'd escaped the causeway and found someplace to rest, she'd been too tired and scared to think it through.

Now she wished they'd kept on going straight to her mom's house and never looked back.

"Show yourself!" The police officer barked out the order.

Laughter from the shadows was the only response.

Brianna twisted on the hood of the Jeep, half-raising

up to speak. "Please, just let us go. We aren't bad kids. We need to get home."

"Be quiet!" The cop shoved Brianna back down.

Madison knew they had to get out of there and away from whoever lurked in the bushes as fast as they could. The longer they stayed vulnerable, the more likely someone would take what they had. Transportation included.

"Identify yourself!" the police officer shouted again.

This time, a figure emerged from the shadows. The beam of light from the flashlight lit up his white tank top and reflected off the metal grip of the handgun tucked in the front of his waistband.

The man had so many tattoos inked up and down his arms and across his back, Madison couldn't tell the color of his skin. But she knew what those types of symbols meant. They were in gang territory.

She shifted on her feet, easing a step closer to the door of the Jeep. There had a be a way out of this where no one got hurt.

The man standing in the pool of light motioned at the cop. "You wanna put that piece down, homeboy? Won't do you no good out here."

"Stand back!" The cop took his hand off Brianna's back to raise the gun once more. His setup was precarious. One hand on a flashlight, one on a handgun. They would be lucky if he didn't accidentally fire a round.

The local took a step forward. "I don't think you heard me, boy. Lower the gun." He patted his own weapon, a smirk twisting up the side of his face. "You don't want to mess with me. I bet you never even fired that thing. Have you?"

The police officer reached for his radio, twisting it on as he spoke into it. "One four six nine requesting backup at Mira Buena Park. Repeat. One four six nine requesting immediate backup."

The radio remained silent.

Madison swallowed. He really didn't know about the EMP. She tried to think. How could they get away?

"We told you the radios don't work. It's just the same emergency alert over and over." Brianna shimmied to get the cop's attention. "You need to let us go."

"Naw. He doesn't need to do any such thing. Ain't that right, bro? You just point that gun at the pretty lady right there and wait for my crew to show up. Then you can go."

"Step back. I told you, I'm calling for backup." The cop tried the radio again. Nothing.

The man in the tank top pulled out his gun before waving it around. "No good, man. Don't you know? Power's out everywhere. One of my guys drove up from LA overnight. Said there's nothing. Hell, I bet even Tijuana's out of power."

With the gun still up in the air, the man took a step forward. "The whole fucking world's powerless. You know what that means?" He pointed the gun at the cop. "Power's mine."

Oh, no. Madison could see it all playing out in slow motion. The shot, the firefight, the collateral damage. She had to stop it. They had to calm the situation down.

"Is the power really out everywhere?" She spoke to

the local, hoping to draw his attention away from the cop long enough to figure out a plan.

He turned to her, tongue running across his lower lip. She fought the urge to recoil. "Hey chica, you so sweet, over there shaking in your boots. You trying to help this sucker out?"

"No. I just—I didn't know. I thought—" She didn't know what to say or do, but she tried to keep talking. Stalling. Anything that could buy them some time.

"Stay away from her." The cop spoke up and Madison whipped her head in his direction. He'd let Brianna go and given her the flashlight.

Both of his hands were wrapped around his gun. "Stay right where you are. You're under arrest."

The man laughed and the sound made Madison's skin crawl. "I don't think you understand who you're talkin' to." He reached for Madison, but she ducked out of his grasp, diving behind the back of the Jeep and out of the direct path of his gun.

The sound of the gunshot pierced the night, so loud Madison's ears rang. Was she shot? She patted herself down. No.

Was it one of her friends? Madison peeked up over the edge of the Jeep. The cop stood still, one hand on his shoulder, fingers red with blood. *Oh, no.*

He motioned toward the Jeep. "Go! Get in the car. I'll hold him off." He fired a shot at the man in the tank top. It missed wide, but the man ducked anyway, taking off for the row of bushes behind them.

Brianna tore open the driver's side door and hollered. "Everybody in. Now!"

Bodies piled into the Jeep as Brianna turned it on and threw it in drive. Peyton landed on top of Madison, his left leg still out of the car as it took off, bumping over the curb before landing with a hard bounce on the concrete.

He tugged the door closed and sat up as Brianna whipped the 4x4 around a corner and punched the gas.

Gunshots rang out behind them. *Rat-a-tat-tat.*

Madison couldn't breathe. She hunched over in a ball, body squeezed down on the floorboard behind Tucker's seat, crammed in with her pack. The tighter she wrapped herself up, the more in control she felt, even though logically she knew it was a lie.

In the span of twelve hours, they'd watched a man bust through a whole bridge full of cars, followed in his wake without stopping to help anyone, got accosted by an overzealous police officer who didn't know the world had ended, almost got killed by a gang member patrolling his turf, and now they were fleeing. *Again.*

All while that cop stayed behind and risked his life. A wave of nausea hit her and she jumped up, rolling down the window just in time to heave over the side of the vehicle. She glanced up, lips slick with spit and bile.

Every house they sped past was dark. Not a light. Not a sound. The whole world was silent except for the sound of the engine and the tires rumbling over the road.

They could have been utterly alone or surrounded by a silent horde. Madison couldn't see much beyond the rooftops, the sky barely lit by dawn.

"Is anyone following us?"

Madison twisted her head, the speed of the car whipping her hair around her face. She pushed it back and peered down the street, squinting to discern any movement in the dark.

After a moment, she fell back onto the seat. "I don't think so. If someone is, they don't have their lights on."

"I didn't hear a car." Tucker pulled his visor down and looked in the mirror. "I think we got away."

Brianna let out a whoop. "Man, what a rush. Did you see the tats on that guy? He'd spent a long time in prison, that's for sure."

Madison wiped at her face. Ever since Tucker had burst into the greenhouse the day before, she hadn't really bought into the science. A little part of her held onto hope. Hope for a mistake, that it wouldn't be as bad as Tucker claimed, that life would still go on and be normal.

Getting shot at and speeding down a dark road just before dawn wasn't normal. Fleeing from a police officer and a gang member wasn't normal. The world would never be normal again.

No more days spent in the warm cocoon of the greenhouse on the UC Davis campus. No more late-night study sessions with bad pizza and a two-liter of soda. She glanced over at Peyton. His dad would never get to launch that record label.

New music. Books. TV shows. Movies. *Gone.*

Hot showers with clean city water. Electricity piped in via wires and transformers. Stoves. Dishwashers. Garbage disposals. *Gone.*

Madison reached for the seatbelt and pulled the thick, sturdy webbing across her lap. Resources were finite. People would figure that out soon.

All the prep she'd done yesterday afternoon seemed so trite now. She hadn't believed Brianna when she'd said to prepare. She hadn't wanted to buy in to Tucker's crazy theories.

But now she didn't have a choice. They were on their own. Even if the government could mobilize, even if the military and police and medical personnel didn't abandon their posts, how long would it last? How long could organized society possibly go on with no internet, no connectivity?

So many people prided themselves on the globalization of society. So many of her professors talked about how the world wasn't one of nations anymore but of people and how eventually, the world would homogenize and there wouldn't be anymore us versus them.

She glanced up at Brianna and Tucker and Peyton. All of that had been a fanciful dream. Now it was the four of them versus everyone else. They had to worry about their own survival.

Everyone else would do the same.

Madison closed her eyes and leaned back on the seat. She wasn't the most religious woman. As soon as she'd gone to college, she'd grown lax in attending church and even praying. But now…

Please, God. Keep my mom and dad safe. Give them a way to survive. Tell them I'm coming. Just as soon as I can.

She blinked her eyes open just in time to catch the first ray of morning sun. She hoped wherever her mom was, that she was staying put. Staying safe.

CHAPTER FIFTEEN

TRACY

S<small>ACRAMENTO</small>, CA
8:30 a.m.

T<small>RACY</small> <small>EASED OUT OF THE GARAGE, BACKING DOWN</small>
the short driveway as she twisted back and forth to
check the street. So far, everything seemed normal.
Wanda sat in the passenger seat, hands in her lap like
usual, staring out the windows with a vacant expression.

Did she always go about life in a cloud? Tracy
couldn't understand how the woman didn't have more
self-awareness. or at least a need for self-preservation.
Maybe she just hadn't been tested.

"Did you grow up here?"

Wanda jumped at Tracy's question out of the blue.
"Does Elk Grove count?"

Tracy frowned. That part of town had to be farm

country when Wanda was young. "Was it built up like it is now?"

Wanda laughed. "Oh, goodness, no. It was us, the chickens, a bunch of alfalfa fields, and that's about it. Our closest neighbor lived a few miles away."

"Have you been down there recently?"

"Mm-hmm." Wanda nodded in slow motion. "The farm we lived on is now an entire subdivision. One hundred and forty houses all on top of each other."

"So did you grow up farming?" If Wanda knew how to tend to crops and animals, she would be invaluable in a future without power.

Wanda palmed her chest. "Me? Not a chance."

"But you lived on a farm."

"We just rented the house on the property. My dad kept the house in order and made repairs, but the big company who owned the farm did all of the work. They shipped in illegals every harvest and cleared that place in a day."

Tracy's hopes fell. "I wish I knew more about agriculture. Madison knows so much, but she's been working on sustainable farming on a large scale. We don't have a big lot. I don't know how much I can convert to a garden or even how much we need."

"You're thinking of gardening?"

Tracy cast a sideways glance at Wanda as she pulled up to an intersection. The lights were out so she waited her turn. "We're going to have to eat somehow."

"Just go to the store. They'll have everything you need."

"How?" Tracy waved around at the intersection and the houses lining the street. "The power's out."

"It'll only be a few days, Tracy. It's not like we've been dropped back in the Stone Age."

That's exactly what it was like, Tracy feared. But Wanda didn't see it.

"Remember that last time? I lost power for three days. So did everyone around me, but they got it back on."

Tracy didn't say anything. She wanted to ask, who is this *they* you keep referencing? The magical people who are going to come and fix everything lickety-split? *They* didn't exist.

Wanda kept making her case. "When Hurricane Sandy hit, people were out of power for almost two weeks. But the Red Cross stepped in and so did FEMA. There weren't any food shortages or riots. Everyone was fine." She straightened up in the seat. "I heard a whole piece on NPR about it."

A shout threatened to bubble up Tracy's throat. Had Wanda not noticed? There wasn't a radio playing in the background in the car. She'd tried it a million times and only got the same emergency alert about severe weather. But this wasn't like a hurricane ripping through or a flood that receded in a few days. This was bigger. Much, much bigger.

She accelerated through the intersection and Wanda pointed up ahead. "See! There's nothing to worry about. Everything will be fine."

Tracy squinted. The gas station she'd thought about the night before sat on the corner, a line of cars already queued up down the street. Tracy pulled in line behind the last one.

"If you don't mind, I'm going to fill up."

"Oh… All right. I guess I can wait to get home. It's not like I have anything to do today."

Tracy ignored the comment and focused on the line in front of her. She counted fifteen cars. Already that many at just after eight in the morning. How long would it take for them to run out of gas? What would people do then?

The car in front of her crept forward and Tracy did the same, both hands on the wheel, eyes and body alert. Giant signs written on cardboard were taped up over the gas station prices.

CASH ONLY
UNLEADED $4.00

"Wow, that's a lot." Wanda stared out the window at the sign. "I wonder why it's so expensive today."

Tracy didn't say a word. The longer they sat in line, the more it reminded her of the highway. If someone tried to break into her vehicle, what would she do? She didn't have a weapon.

At least this time she didn't have anything to steal in the back.

They inched forward, a car at a time, until only three cars separated them from the pumps. It had taken almost an hour.

Wanda fidgeted, checking her hair in the mirror, rifling through her purse, popping a mint in her mouth.

Tracy's stomach rumbled. She should have eaten more before they left, but she'd wanted to be done and back home by now. Every minute she stayed away from home and the supplies made her nervous.

A commotion up front caught her attention. A man stood beside his convertible, arm waving a credit card in the gas station employee's face. Tracy cracked her window to hear.

"I don't care that you want cash only. I don't have any and I need gas. I'm running on damn fumes. You're the only gas station open for forty miles!"

The employee, a middle-aged man with a beer belly and a stoic expression, crossed his arms. "The credit card machines don't work. It's cash or nothing."

Mr. Convertible didn't appreciate the response. He slammed the door to his car and stomped up to the employee before jabbing the credit card forward. He poked the employee right in the center of his button-down work shirt.

The man didn't even flinch.

Tracy tightened her grip on the steering wheel.

"What on earth is the holdup?"

"The customer doesn't have any cash."

"Then he should pay with a credit card."

"The machines are down. The gas station won't take them."

Wanda let out a *pfft*. "That's nonsense. They've got power. The machines probably work just fine. He's just being a jerk."

Tracy kept her mouth shut. She didn't need to argue

with Wanda; she needed to keep an eye on the scene playing out in front of them.

A vehicle behind Mr. Convertible, one of those enormous battering-ram luxury SUVs, eased forward, horn blaring. The man trying to get gas flipped the driver the bird and kept arguing.

"Just take my damn card and give me some gas!"

The employee stood there, unmoving. A tremor of fear skittered down Tracy's spine.

The woman in the monster SUV rolled down the window and stuck her head out. "Get out of the way, you asshole! We're late for school!"

Oh, no.

"What did you just call me?" The man spun around before taking a step toward the woman.

"Are you going to move or what?"

"I'm not moving until this son of a bitch lets me buy some gas."

Wanda looked over at Tracy. "Do you think we should offer to help? We could pay for his gas."

Tracy frowned. "With the price so high, I don't even think I have enough cash to fill up the tank. Do you have any? Maybe together we could—"

Wanda shook her head, cutting Tracy off before she could finish. "I never keep cash. Find it a waste of time, really. Everywhere takes cards."

"Then I guess we aren't offering anything."

Wanda opened her mouth to argue, but Tracy faced the windshield. At this point, the man had turned back to the employee, but the soccer mom with a bad attitude just wouldn't quit.

She laid on the horn again, easing her giant boat of a vehicle forward. *She can't be. Please tell me… Oh, no.*

Tracy clenched her teeth together, bracing for the worst.

She heard the collision before she saw it, the crunching sound of bumpers buckling rising to meet her ears while time seemed to slow to a crawl.

The angry customer's mouth contorted, his eyes screwed up, and his cheeks flamed. He watched as the SUV hit his precious convertible, the power roof mangling into a half-up, half-down position as the woman kept going.

He raced toward the car, throwing open the passenger door as the woman behind him backed up, ready to hit him again.

The gun went off before Tracy even recognized the black shape in the man's hand. Mr. Convertible came armed to the gas station. His first shot missed the SUV completely, most likely due to his anger and not his ability to aim.

The woman screamed, bloodcurdling and loud, and punched the gas, sideswiping Mr. Convertible's car as she tried to get away. He fired after her, one bullet piercing the back window and shattering the glass.

Other drivers began to move, some tearing out from behind Tracy in line, others backing up and trying to get away before the angry man turned his sights on them.

Tracy didn't move.

"What are you doing? We need to get out of here!" Wanda shrieked from a crouch on the seat, her body contorted into a lumpy ball as she hid from the chaos.

Tracy didn't panic. If anything, she hyper-focused, time slowing to a speed where she could process the whole scene. She turned to Wanda. "We're not leaving. We need gas."

"You're insane!"

"No. I'm realistic." She turned back to the front in time to see the employee emerge from the store, shotgun in his hands. He must have run back inside when the shooting started. He racked it and pointed it straight at the man holding the handgun.

"Lower the gun and leave or I'll pump enough buckshot to turn you into a damn human doily!"

The man holding the handgun hesitated, whipping his head back and forth as he looked for a way out. There wasn't one. He must have known the odds.

After a moment, he lowered the gun, muttering beneath his breath. He walked around the car and tugged open the driver's side door before sliding into the seat.

"What's happening?"

"*Shhh.*" Tracy couldn't manage Wanda and the situation. She watched as the man turned on his car and revved the engine. He peeled out, bumping over the curb and scraping the bottom of his car as he hit the street.

In seconds he was gone and the whole incident was over. Tracy exhaled. She was the only car left.

She pulled up to the gas pump and turned off the engine. Wanda still cowered in the seat beside her, refusing to sit up and look around. Tracy got out and made her way over to the employee who still held the shotgun in both hands.

Holding five twenties out in front of her, Tracy smiled. "Hi, there. Can I get however much a hundred dollars will buy me?"

The employee's face relaxed and he exhaled. "Of course, ma'am. For you, I'll even knock off fifty cents a gallon."

CHAPTER SIXTEEN

TRACY

Sacramento, CA
  10:30 a.m.

Tracy tried the radio for the tenth time, rolling the dial up and down. Nothing but static. She clicked it off.

Not knowing what really happened... Not being able to contact her family... Not hearing a single word from any Federal, State, or local government... It all took a toll.

Instead of hunkering down and staying put, she'd driven across town to help a virtual stranger do... what, exactly? Check on her house? Get dropped off? She didn't even know. She needed to set the record straight sooner rather than later. Wanda could stay with Tracy if she agreed to contribute, but she needed to face reality, and quick.

Soft-pedaling around the facts and trying to make Wanda comfortable would only hurt them both in the long run. Tracy rubbed her temple, fighting back a tension headache, as Wanda pointed ahead.

"That's my complex just ahead on the right."

Golden Acres Active Senior Community.

Tracy glanced at Wanda. "You live in a retirement community?"

Wanda shrugged, her smile a bit sheepish. "They've got good amenities. A cafeteria, organized events. It's nice."

The Suburban eased over the curb and Wanda *tsked* out loud. "I hate it when they leave the gates open."

Tracy almost volunteered the obvious comment about the lack of power, but she bit her tongue instead. Wanda still didn't seem to have a grasp on anything approaching reality. Were other people as clueless as the head librarian or was she an outlier?

A man with a clipboard and a harried expression flagged them down. Tracy pulled into a parking spot in front of what looked like the manager's office and rolled down her window.

The man couldn't have been older than thirty, but the day-old stubble on his jaw and the bags under his eyes aged him a decade or more. He'd been busy.

"I know the gates aren't working, but this is a closed community. Residents and guests only." He glanced down at his clipboard. "Who are you here to—" He stopped mid-question when Wanda leaned forward and waved.

"Hey, Dave!"

"Oh, Wanda! Thank God you're all right." Dave exhaled, hand on his chest for emphasis. "I can take you off the missing list." He flipped a page on the clipboard and made a note.

Wanda motioned for Tracy to turn off the car and get out. Part of her wanted to decline and leave Wanda to whatever she'd find at the apartment complex. But the good-hearted part of her couldn't. If they needed help, she could assist for a few hours at least.

They both stepped out of the Suburban and Tracy locked the doors. She held out her hand. "Tracy Sloane. I work with Wanda at the library."

"Dave Andrews." He took her hand and pumped it up and down. "I'm the general manager. It's been one hell of a twenty-four hours."

"What's going on?" Wanda stood next to Tracy, hand up to her eyes to shield them from the morning sun as she looked around.

"What isn't?" Dave looked down at his sheet. "When the power went out it was like a…" he glanced around, trying to come up with the words, "…surge. Everything got brighter, a microwave in the breakroom exploded, the transformer out front burst into flames. It was chaos."

Wanda glanced around. "Did the fire department come? Did they put out the fires?"

"No. I can't make a single call. The landlines are down. There's no cell service. No one even knows where the closest fire department is. But that's not the worst of it."

He paled as he spoke, the clipboard in his hand shaking enough for Tracy to notice.

"What's the worst?" Tracy asked.

He ran a hand down his face, fingers pausing to rub at his lips. "We're lost fourteen residents already. Ten more are critical and probably won't last another day."

"What? How?" Wanda's mouth gaped in shock, her blue eyes as wide as the ocean.

Dave swallowed. "Eight had pacemakers. Something about the power outage… It wrecked them."

Tracy nodded. It made sense when she thought about it. "A lot of modern pacemakers are actually controlled via wireless technology. They use the same cell network or satellites that our phones and TV use. Without power, the central monitoring facility is down. There's no one telling those pacemakers what to do."

"Oh my goodness." Wanda smacked her lips, opening and shutting her mouth like a guppy.

Dave nodded. "We've got other patients on home oxygen. Without power, we can't keep those systems running."

"What about portable oxygen? Don't you have some?"

"We do, and they're all being used." Dave glanced down at the ground. "There weren't enough portable machines for everyone."

Wanda raised her hands, waving them in front of her like she could wipe everything Dave said away. "What about the backup generators?"

Dave kicked at a broken piece of asphalt in front of

him. "They only support the main building. Not the residences." He looked up, eyes pained. "Not that it matters, anyway. The generators will run out of gas tonight. I sent Monica out this morning to find more fuel, but she said every gas station she drove by was closed. There's no diesel to be had."

He glanced at his watch. "We've got maybe four more hours. Then the refrigerators and freezers in the cafeteria will start to defrost. We'll lose all the food in cold storage."

Tracy closed her eyes for a moment. *This is real. Everything I feared, everything Joe and I discussed… It's all real.*

She had to admit that although she thought Wanda was delusional, the woman's unflagging optimism in society had gotten to Tracy. She'd begun to doubt her own cynicism.

Wanda turned to look at the mostly empty parking lot. "Where's all the staff? The nurses, cooks… They should be here."

"No nurses showed up this morning. It's me and Monica and Edgar in grounds maintenance. That's it."

"How many residents do you have?" Tracy almost hated to ask, but she couldn't help it. She had to know.

Dave's lips thinned into a line. "Living? One hundred and eighty-six."

"How many can make it through the night?"

He glanced down at his clipboard, flipping the first two pages. Tracy saw big red X marks over a handful of names and question marks next to so many more.

"We'll probably lose twenty or thirty by morning. If the power stays out…" He trailed off, not willing to face the horror. "I'm keeping a list. Dead, dying, and missing. I've got about thirty residents I can't find. One less now that Wanda's here." He gave her a forlorn, broken smile.

Tracy fought the urge to reach out and hug the man. He didn't need comfort. He needed assistance on a massive scale. Assistance that probably would never come.

"Where are the police? The ambulances? Shouldn't someone have come by now?" Wanda's voice had taken on an almost ephemeral quality, there and gone before anyone could blink.

"No one's coming. Edgar made it in this morning, but he said it was bad downtown. Riots, looting. He said he heard more gunshots than he could count."

"Already? But the power's only been out a day!"

"Not even. Word is that the gangs don't think it's ever coming back on. They're seizing territory, throwing people out of their homes, ransacking stores. With phones not working and those emergency alerts they keep blasting out, it's causing panic. Chaos." Dave shook his head. "It's like they think it's judgment day or something. Edgar said he heard chants of '*Our Time*' over and over as he drove through."

"It's a wonder he made it out of there alive." Tracy was surprised. If it had already gotten that bad in parts of the city, how long before the crime wave spread?

Dave nodded. "Tell me about it. He claims it's because he drives a POS car. No one wanted it."

Tracy snorted back a smile. Edgar seemed like a good guy to get to know.

Wanda peered behind her at the building across the parking lot. "Is it safe to go to my place?"

Dave nodded. "Just watch your step. The hallways are dark. Oh, and the water's off now, too. So don't use the toilet."

Tracy hesitated. She wished there was something she could do for Dave other than wish him good luck. But she knew there was nothing. Helping would only prolong the inevitable. She needed to get back home to protect her supplies and wait for her family.

They would be coming. She knew it.

Wanda smiled at Dave. "Thank you."

"Of course. Sorry I can't do more."

Wanda turned toward her building and Tracy followed a step behind. The entire walk across the parking lot she thought about Dave's information. No police, no fire department. No military to speak of.

They were on their own. Maybe for good.

Wanda pulled open the glass door to the building and stepped over the brick that had been used to prop it ajar. As soon as she stepped inside, a stench hit Tracy's nose and she gagged.

"What is that?" Wanda looked like she might throw up.

"I don't want to know. Let's just get to your place."

Wanda pointed as she held her other hand up to her nose to block some of the smell. "It's down here."

They walked in silence, both breathing through their mouths and fighting the urge to retch.

Wanda stopped in front of a door and fished her

keys out of her purse. She stuck one in the lock, turned the knob, and shoved the door open.

One step inside and she dropped her purse on the floor. "What the…?"

CHAPTER SEVENTEEN

MADISON

West Sacramento, CA
10:00 a.m.

"Let's face it. We're lost." Tucker leaned back in his seat, chewing on the end of his pen as he scanned the street.

"No, we're not." Brianna shook her curls at him. "We're just… taking the long way."

Peyton grumbled from the back seat. "We've been driving for hours and getting nowhere."

Brianna gesticulated at the windows. "It's not my fault half the roads are blocked and we have to turn around."

"How much gas do we have left, anyway?"

She glanced at the gauge. "Enough."

Madison stifled a yawn. "Let's pull over and take a

break. My legs are so stiff I might fall over when I stand up."

Tucker pointed his chewed-up pen out the window. "How about that shopping center? Maybe someone can give us directions."

Madison didn't think talking to strangers was a good idea, but she needed to get out of the car and walk around.

Brianna slowed the Jeep. "Fine. But we're not staying longer than we have to. I want to get Madison home ASAP."

Tucker glanced over at his girlfriend. Madison didn't miss the tension radiating between them. Although Brianna was dead set on high-tailing it up to her family cabin north of Truckee, Tucker didn't seem so enthusiastic.

"We might want to stay the night. Regroup, eat, get a good night's sleep. Who knows what the roads will be like. The highway could be jammed."

Brianna scowled, refusing to buy in to Tucker's theories. She parked away from the other handful of cars in the parking lot and turned off the engine.

It was a typical strip mall in this part of town, complete with a Metro PCS, minimart, and a payday loans store. Two of the three were now worthless. But the minimart could be filled to the brim with shelf-stable food and supplies. They catered to not only locals without a car who relied on the shop for their daily groceries, but also to motorists buzzing by who needed something quickly.

It would have antifreeze and batteries. Flashlights and motor oil.

Madison eyed the front doors. "You think anyone's working the minimart today?"

"Are you crazy? The whole world's gone to shit. You really think someone's going to be in there selling Twinkies?"

"I'd be more worried about who else has the same idea." Peyton nodded at the cluster of other cars parked in the lot. "Look."

Madison leaned closer to the window to watch. While they had pulled into the parking space, four men had congregated at the far corner of the lot, heads together, talking. All clad in jeans and loose T-shirts, none looked up to any good. One held a baseball bat loose at his side, almost invisible when he tucked it against his pants.

"Are they about to break in?"

"I don't know. Maybe."

Madison sat up with a start. "We should go. If they're about to rob the place, we don't want to get caught up in that."

Tucker shifted in his seat. "They can't take everything."

"What are you talking about?"

"The minimart's got to have a ton of stuff. Food, water, beer. We could wait them out. When they leave, we can go in and scoop up what's left."

Madison gawked. "That's stealing."

Peyton nodded. "Madison's right. We can't just go in there and take what doesn't belong to us."

"You really think anyone's going to care?"

"The minimart owner will. What happens when he comes back and there's nothing left of his store?"

"If it's not us, it'll be someone else. How long do you think any of the leftovers will last? It's not like we're the ones doing the smashing." Tucker hesitated. "Just the grabbing."

Madison shook her head. She couldn't believe what he was saying. "So that makes it right? We weren't the first? Someone else will do it, why not us? Do you even hear yourself?"

"*Shhh.*" Brianna motioned for everyone to be quiet. "They're looking at us."

Madison and Peyton ducked down in the back seat. With the tinted windows, Madison wasn't even sure the men could see in, but she wasn't taking any chances. "Do they see us?"

"I don't know. But they're pointing and talking." Tucker turned to Brianna. "We should get out of here."

"And miss a chance for some junk food? The bag sitting in there might be the last jalapeño Doritos we'll ever have the chance to eat."

"You seriously want to risk death for chips that give you nasty breath?" Peyton shook his head as he looked at Madison. "Your roommate is certifiable."

"Hey! This roommate is your ride. Watch it, buddy."

"Shit. Brianna, let's go. They're moving."

She peered over Tucker's shoulder before grabbing him by the face. "Quick, kiss me."

"What? No!"

"Just do it. Make out. Look convincing." Brianna

yanked on Tucker, but he refused to budge. After a moment, she cursed and climbed over him, tearing off her jacket to expose a trim little tank top.

"Brianna, stop it!"

"No. If they think we just pulled in here to get it on, they'll leave us alone."

"You can't be serious. Where did you come up with this idea?"

She pulled the ponytail holder out of her hair and tossed her curls around, pretending to come on to him. "In a movie. Come on. Kiss me."

Tucker groaned and reached up for Brianna, dragging her down for a kiss. All the while he mumbled against her lips. "This is the stupidest idea you've ever had, babe."

"Shut up!" Brianna leaned in and squished her chest against Tucker's. "What are they doing now?" She hissed her question into the backseat as she pretended to kiss Tucker's neck.

Madison stared out the window, her face barely sticking up over the edge of the door panel. "They're watching… And pointing… And…" Madison cleared her throat. "Making some lewd gestures."

Peyton snorted next to her, still couched down below the windows.

"And now they're turning around and heading back to the store."

"See. I told you this would work." Brianna stayed put, straddling Tucker as the four men regrouped in front of the minimart. Never once did she look up, relying instead on Madison's play-by-play.

"All right. I think they're about to bust in." Madison tensed, every muscle in her body coiled tight. She was watching a crime. A bunch of thugs who one day into the apocalypse wanted nothing more than to smash and grab.

She glanced up at her roommate and her boyfriend, still pretending to get it on in the front seat. Were they any different? They didn't have a baseball bat and a bad attitude, but Tucker wanted to break in. Brianna agreed.

If the power never came back on, how long before everyone turned into a thug with a bat and a bad attitude?

The sound of shattering glass made Madison jump. The man with the bat hit the front door again and again, knocking out giant shards of glass. It didn't seem real.

He shouted at his buddies and one after another they hopped through the debris and disappeared inside.

Madison exhaled. Brianna sat up.

"Aw, come on, I was kinda getting into that."

Brianna raised an eyebrow at her boyfriend. "The whole risk of possible death didn't kill your libido?"

He held up his hands with a grin. "I'm a nineteen-year-old guy, Brianna. What do you think?"

Peyton laughed in the backseat, and Tucker reached out to high five.

A gunshot cut the joking short. All four college students turned toward the store. Another shot. Shouts. More gunfire. How many guns did they have in there?

Everyone in the Jeep started talking at once.

"What's happening?"

"I don't know."

"We should go."

Brianna slid off Tucker and back into the driver's seat. "If there's a gun, we're out." She went to start the car when Tucker grabbed her arm. "Get down!"

Everyone hunched down in their seats except Madison. She kept watch from her crouch. One of the criminals staggered out of the store, gripping his belly. His white T-shirt bloomed red with blood.

"Oh my God." Brianna's whisper broke the silence. "Was he shot?"

Madison nodded. "I think so. Where are the others?"

Just as she asked the question, another man ducked and ran from the building carrying a case of beer under each arm.

Madison and her friends stared out the windows, waiting and watching. After what seemed like forever, Madison sat up. "I don't think anyone else is coming out."

"We should go." Tucker reached for his seatbelt, but Madison shook her head.

"No. We need to get in there."

"What? You're the one who complained that we were breaking the law. Now you want to pillage around a couple dead bodies?"

She didn't want to do anything of the sort. But while they'd been sitting there, she'd realized what else the minimart would have. Madison glanced up at Brianna. "We need to go in. That place will have a map."

Tucker cursed under his breath.

"Madison's right." Peyton cast her a look. "We need to figure out how to get to her house from here."

Brianna protested. "We can find the highway, I know it. As soon as we do, Madison can get us home."

"What if the highway's blocked? We've been trying that for hours anyway. How long do you want to keep going in circles?" Tucker sat up. "Think about it. What if we need to take back roads up to your parents' place? We need a map."

"You seriously want to go in there?" Brianna stared at her boyfriend, eyes wide with disbelief.

"No. But we need to." Tucker unlocked the doors and pushed his open. "Who's coming with me?"

CHAPTER EIGHTEEN

MADISON

West Sacramento, CA
11:00 a.m.

"What if whoever shot that guy is still in there?"

Madison glanced over at Peyton and shrugged. "We'll just have to call out. Tell him we're not there to rob him."

"And if he shoots at us?"

"Duck?" She knew it wasn't a good answer, but what choice did they have? They needed a map. Based on all the gunfire, she didn't think anyone could still be alive inside, but it wasn't like she had a lot of experience.

Madison wished her father was there. He'd know exactly what to do. She reached for Peyton's hand and gave it a squeeze.

He shook his head. "This is nuts even if it is the end of the world."

Tucker reached the front door first with Brianna just behind. He called out. "Hello? Is anyone in there? Do you need medical assistance? Hello?"

They waited in the silence.

"We can help you! Hello?"

"We can't help anybody. What are you doing?" Brianna chastised her boyfriend as she stood just outside the door, body tucked against a slim portion of brick wall.

"I'm getting them to trust us. But I don't think I need to. Come on." Tucker stepped into the store and Madison's heart thudded against her chest in frantic alarm.

She'd never done anything like this. No breaking in, no sneaking around. She'd been the good kid. The model student. She glanced at Brianna, who eased in behind Tucker with a steeled expression. Now she wished she'd been a bit more like her roommate.

Brave. Daring. Maybe even reckless. She'd have faced more fear. Been more prepared for the end of the world.

Tucker called out from inside the store. "It's all right. Looks like they're all dead."

Madison exhaled a shaky breath and turned to Peyton. "You or me? Who's standing guard outside?"

Peyton glanced at the empty street and back at Madison. "If you don't mind, I think I'll stay out here. The smell of blood always makes me nauseous."

She nodded and ducked into the store, sidestepping

the giant piles of broken glass. Telling Peyton he might have to get over that problem wouldn't help right now, but it was true. They'd all have to grow up, and quick.

Blinking in an attempt to adjust to the dim light in the store, Madison took stock. The gunfight had taken place in the middle, leaving the side aisles untouched. They looked like any other convenience store in any other town.

A drinks station with coffee and soda and frozen slushes. A microwave and a spot for rolling hotdogs and hanging pretzels. An entire wall of beer going bad in refrigerators that might never turn on again.

The only thing different was this one had blood and glass and two dead bodies. Madison swallowed. The first robber lay face down, a pool of blood hugging his chest. It had this sheen to it already, like milk with a skin. If she touched it, it would probably be tacky.

Madison tried not to think about the reality of the moment. A dead man right in front of her. She eased around his body, thankful she couldn't see his face. She wasn't as lucky the second time.

The other thief sat slumped over by the candy bar shelf, one hand in his lap like he'd died clutching his gut. The gunshot had torn through him, ripping his middle open as it sent him to the floor.

She glanced up. "Have you found a shotgun? That's the only thing that could make these wounds."

Tucker popped up from the chips aisle, his mouth puffed up like a chipmunk. "Swrrwy... Gwt dswrctwd."

"You're stuffing your face?" Brianna emerged from

behind the counter. "We're standing in a store that just got robbed and you're stuffing your face with what?"

Tucker held up the bag and shrugged.

Jalapeño Doritos.

Brianna groaned. "That better not be the last bag." She turned to Madison and held up a shotgun with one hand and a box of shells with the other. "Guy had some serious buckshot back here. No wonder those two look like hamburger."

A wave of nausea rose up Madison's throat, but she pushed it down. No time to get sick. Everyone dealt with death in a different way. Brianna joked it off, Tucker stuffed his face, Peyton stayed outside. Madison could stand there, staring at the dead man beside her all day, thinking about life and death and what it all meant, but it wouldn't get her anything except possibly the same fate.

"Hey. Are you all right?"

Madison glanced up at Brianna and nodded. "Yeah. I just need to get out of my own head."

"Do that and grab whatever we might need, okay?"

Madison nodded. "Where's the owner?"

Brianna shrugged. "Beats me. Maybe he ran out the back." She glanced around at the floor. "I'm looking for another gun. From all the shots we heard, there has to be a handgun around here somewhere." Brianna scowled at Tucker. "And you. Worthless excuse for a boyfriend. Get some shopping bags and fill them with whatever you can. Food, batteries, flashlights. Motor oil if they have it."

Tucker shoved the last chip in his mouth and nodded. "Yes, ma'am."

Madison rolled her eyes. Tucker might have risked his life for a bag of Doritos and a box of Slim Jim's, but Madison risked her life for one thing: a map.

While the other two searched and collected, Madison scanned the store, looking for the familiar little carousel. *Bingo!* It was tucked in the back, wedged between the ATM machine and the bathrooms.

She rushed up to it, spinning the sections around as she plucked every map they could possibly need off the tines. Madison clutched them all in her hands and said a silent thank you to whomever might be listening. They could make it home. In a few hours, she'd see her mom, hopefully her dad, and they could relax.

Sleep.

She eyed the cookies behind her. Eat some junk. Madison grabbed a bag of Oreos and headed toward the door. Brianna stood one aisle over, staring down at the floor. Madison made her way to her.

The thug she'd passed by before still sat in the same place, hand in his lap, Twix and Snickers cascading like a frozen waterfall down his shoulders. "What is it?"

Brianna held up a blood-covered handgun. Large, with what appeared to be metal insets and scrollwork, the gun had to cost a small fortune. "He made a point of carrying a show piece." Brianna shook her head. "Lot of good it did him."

"Maybe that's all it was. He might not have even known how to shoot it."

Brianna nodded. "You're probably right." She

ejected the magazine and checked the chamber with a snort. "He didn't even have a round in the chamber." Brianna shook her head. "We're barely two days into this thing, whatever it is, and these idiots get themselves shot."

"Your point?"

"How many more are going to be just like them? How many people are going to totally lose their minds and get themselves killed?"

"More than we can count." Madison reached out and rubbed Brianna's shoulder. "Come on, we should go."

Brianna nodded. "Thanks for coming with me."

Madison smiled. "Thanks for driving."

"Dude. They've got Ho Hos!"

Both girls rolled their eyes and laughed. Leave it to Tucker to break the tension. They might be standing over a dead body holding guns and priceless maps, but Tucker still cracked them up.

"Let's go, Ho Ho man. We're done."

"Aw, come on. There's so much stuff here…"

"Now, Tucker."

"Fine." He emerged from the aisle, arms laden with a million bags, each one stuffed to the brim with cookies and chips and sodas. "I can't carry any more anyway."

Madison laughed to herself and followed Brianna and Tucker out of the store. The sunlight almost blinded her. "Hold on! We need one more thing." She rushed back in and grabbed the first four sunglasses on the rack by the door.

"Eye protection." She handed them out as all four college friends walked toward the Jeep.

Peyton popped on a reflective pair of aviators. "How do I look?"

"Very Judgment Day."

He grinned. "How was the store?"

"Be glad you missed it."

He nodded as they stopped outside the car. Tucker piled his bags into the already overloaded back while Peyton and Madison climbed in the back seat.

Once they all made it inside, Brianna turned on the engine. "All right. Where to now?"

Madison grinned as she unfolded a map of the greater Sacramento area. "Home. Now we're going home."

Brianna backed out of the space and eased up to the street. "Which way?"

"Just a second." Madison found their location on the map and her parents' house. They were still over twenty miles away. They'd have never made it home by dark without a map. She exhaled with relief and gratitude. Sometimes the worst situations turned out to be the best.

She pointed out the window. "Take a left at the light."

Brianna pulled out onto the street. In an hour, they'd be home. Madison hoped she'd find everything she needed, including her parents, safe and sound.

CHAPTER NINETEEN

TRACY

Sacramento, CA
  10:30 a.m.

"I take it you didn't leave it like this."

Wanda shook her head, tears welling in her eyes as she surveyed the destruction. "No."

A coffee table stood on its side in the living room; magazines that once perched on top now littered the floor. Drawers from a corner desk lay about like lazy cats on the rug in front of the window, catching the morning sun. Every single kitchen cabinet door hung open, shelves mucked about and contents ransacked.

It looked like a scene from a movie, the one right before the bad guy rushed out from the bedroom and did the homeowner in. Tracy crept down the hall. *Please have no one be here. Please.*

She nudged open a door with her hiking boot. Bathroom, empty. On down the hall she went. Checking in every closet before the last door. With a deep breath, she turned the handle and pushed it open. *Thank God.*

Wanda's bedroom sat empty and relatively undisturbed. Whomever tossed the place either ran out of time or figured she didn't have anything worth stealing in there. With a bed covered in a pink fluffy comforter and a wall of bookcases stuffed to the gills with books, Tracy was surprised.

Guess the thief wasn't a reader.

She made her way back out to the main rooms and found Wanda crouched on the floor in the living room, holding two pieces of a figurine. Tears streaked her cheeks. "My mother gave this to me for my sixteenth birthday." She snuffed back snot and held up the two pieces, fitting them together as best she could. A ballerina with a broken leg. "When I was young, I wanted to be a dancer."

Tracy knelt beside her. "I'm sorry." She rubbed the older woman's back, trying to comfort her. Tracy didn't know what to do. She needed to get home, quickly. Every minute she stayed with Wanda meant another minute her home sat unprotected.

What if Madison made it home and she wasn't there? Or Walter showed up and feared the worst?

Part of her wanted to leave Wanda to fend for herself. But how could she leave her here in the midst of all this destruction?

Tracy stood up and walked over to the sliding door. It stood open about an inch without any kind of backstop. Anyone could hop the railing to Wanda's patio and walk on in. Wanda couldn't have been that reckless. Could she?

"Did you leave your sliding door open?"

Wanda wiped at an eye and sniffed back another wave of tears. "I always leave it open a crack. It lets the air in."

Tracy closed her eyes and pinched the bridge of her nose. Lashing out in anger wasn't her style, but even she could be driven to the breaking point. "You can't just leave your doors and windows unlocked. Anyone could have just come on in and helped themselves."

"But this is a gated community."

"Not anymore."

Wanda stood up, cradling the figurine in her hands. "We have a security guard who drives around on a golf cart. Everyone talks about how safe they feel here. I've never had to worry. I just don't understand why a person would do this."

Something inside Tracy snapped. She'd tried for the past twenty-four hours to treat Wanda with kid gloves, to ease her into the new reality they faced. But screw it. The woman needed to face reality, or best-case scenario, she'd be dead soon. Worst case, she'd bring Tracy along for the ride.

Tracy dropped her hand. "When are you going to wake up? The world has changed, Wanda. It's not like it was before. It never will be."

"You don't know that."

"Look around you! You think this is a one-time thing? Everyone has to fend for themselves. Protect themselves. There won't be any aid. The government won't be swooping in here with food and water and the power company."

"Yes, they will. It might take a few days, but the power always comes back on."

Tracy stalked up to Wanda, ready to shake some sense into her. "The grid can't come back from a CME. The type of EMP it released fried the grid. We don't have the means to bring it back. I explained all of this already."

Wanda sniffed. "I thought you were being dramatic."

Tracy palmed her hips and stayed silent, not trusting herself to speak. Anger and frustration filled her. Anger at the woman standing in front of her, the inability of her fellow citizens to prepare or even grasp something like this might happen, at her government for failing to appreciate the risks.

There were so many people she could direct all those pent-up emotions toward, but it wouldn't do any good. She'd be shouting in a padded room. No one could help her now but herself.

Wanda set the broken ballerina on her fireplace mantel and wiped her palms down the front of her dress. "I'm sorry I haven't been much help since you picked me up."

Tracy exhaled and managed a nod.

"I guess I thought…" She paused and looked around her. "If I ignored everything you said, then it couldn't be real. I'd get back here and it would be just like I left it. The power would be on, the water would be running, and I could go back to my life." She tucked a flyaway bit of hair behind her ear. "Silly, huh?"

Tracy's anger dissipated like helium out of a leaky balloon. "Infuriating, actually."

Wanda cracked a smile. "I'm sorry, Tracy."

"It's okay." Tracy ran her tongue across her lips before continuing. "Look, Wanda. I know this is all hard for you to accept."

"I'm beginning to."

"That's good. But it takes more than that."

"What are you saying?"

Tracy perched on the edge of the couch arm and motioned at the destruction all around them. "This is the world now. It's only going to get worse." She paused, trying to gauge Wanda's reaction. "Are you going to do what it takes to survive or not?"

Wanda's brows knit together. "Like what?"

"Learn skills, persevere when things get tough, not let setbacks do you in."

"You mean like this?"

"Mm-hmm. But that's just the start. If this is the new normal, we can't depend on anyone for anything. No stores, no police, no trash pickup." Tracy leaned in. "No hospitals, no gas stations, no electric company. Just us and our skills."

Wanda wiped at her face, drying her tears and rubbing some color back in her cheeks. "Okay. I get it."

"Good." Tracy stood up. "Get dressed into something more practical. I'll start collecting anything we can use."

Wanda blinked. "What are you saying?"

Tracy didn't hesitate. "I'm taking you back home. You can stay with me."

The hug caught Tracy off guard. Wanda wrapped her thick arms around her, squeezing until Tracy almost squeaked. Her sweater muffled Wanda's voice, but Tracy heard her anyway. "Thank you. I don't know what I would have done if you hadn't seen me waiting for the bus." Wanda gave her another squeeze before pulling back.

Tracy appreciated the gesture, but words didn't mean as much as action. Not now, anyway. "Don't thank me yet. We've got a lot of work to do."

Wanda nodded. "I know. I'll do my share."

I hope so. Tracy flashed her a tight smile. "Is it okay if I start in the kitchen?"

"Of course. I'll change and see what I can find in the bedroom. Anything you think we might need, please take it."

"Will do." Tracy waited until Wanda disappeared down the hall before turning around. She didn't know if the woman could deliver on her promises, but it was a start. Offering whatever supplies she had on hand meant something, too. Her kitchen might not have much, but there had to be a few things they could use.

Tracy opened cabinets and peered past plates and cups. She yanked open drawers and rifled through silverware and baking supplies. Wanda didn't have much in the way of end-of-the-world preparedness. A roll of duct tape shoved in the back of the junk drawer and a pack of AA batteries would come in handy. Tracy set them on the counter.

The flashlight and fire extinguisher under the sink, along with most of the cleaning supplies, could be useful. She added them to the pile before opening the cabinet above the sink. Vitamins and medicine. Tracy didn't bother to read the labels, opting instead to scoop everything up in her arms and dump them in an empty recycling container she'd found under the sink.

She opened the next cabinet. The pantry. All the food that wasn't already rotten would come with them. Crackers and chips and cereal would only last so long, but food was food. She piled it all on top of the vitamins before reaching for the stool tucked in the corner.

Tracy stepped on top of it and almost let out a whoop when she saw what sat on the second shelf. An almost-full case of Slim Fast in cans. Dieting had never been her thing. Tracy preferred to sweat off her calories with a good run or a lifting session at her gym. But Slim Fast was intended as meal replacement. It could get them through hard times.

She tugged the partially wrapped case off the shelf and climbed down before setting it on the counter.

"I've never been very good at sticking to a diet. Those things taste like chalk."

Tracy spun around and gawked. The woman standing in front of her barely looked like the Wanda she knew. Instead of a flowy skirt and loose hair, Wanda had changed into hiking gear: jeans, boots, and a T-shirt. With her graying hair in a braid she looked like a plump Jane Goodall, ready to set off for a trek through the misty mountains.

"Wow, Wanda, I didn't think…"

She shrugged when Tracy ran out of words. "I took up hiking a few years ago. A bunch of us old gals get together once a month and do a day hike in the area."

"Great." Tracy motioned at the things she'd piled on the counter. "I've pulled just about everything out of the kitchen we can use."

Wanda nodded. "I packed a bag of clothes and grabbed some wool blankets I had in the closet. There's a suitcase full of toiletries by the bathroom door, too."

Tracy marveled. An hour ago she'd never thought Wanda would be capable of getting anything together, let alone actually helping. Maybe the woman wasn't a lost cause.

"And there's this." Wanda set her bag down and pulled out a zippered pouch. She opened it and held it out to Tracy.

A revolver sat inside, along with a handful of bullets. Tracy blinked. Wanda owned a gun?

"It was my father's. When he died, I kept it. But I don't know the first thing about guns." She puffed up her cheeks as she thought. "I don't think it's been fired in thirty years."

Tracy reached out. "May I?"

Wanda nodded and Tracy picked up the revolver, squinting to read the engraving on the side. *COLT. D.A. 45. UNITED STATES PROPERTY.* The bottom of the grip had another inscription, *U.S. ARMY MODEL 1917.* Tracy glanced up. "Was your father in the war?"

Wanda nodded. "He enlisted in '41 when he was only 17. Lied a bit about his age to get in."

Tracy nodded. She didn't know much about World War II history, but a gun was a gun. "I'm surprised they issued him a revolver. Seems like by then it would have been all rifles and semi-automatic pistols."

Wanda's brows pinched together. "I want to say he traded for it, but I don't remember the details. My dad never liked talking about the war. Every time I'd ask, he'd change the topic."

Tracy nodded. Her uncle had been the same way. "Do you have any more ammunition?"

Wanda shook her head.

Tracy picked up one of the rounds and rolled it in her fingers. Six wasn't a lot, but it was better than none. She zipped the case back up and handed it back to Wanda. "Put this somewhere safe and let's get out of here."

Wanda slid the pouch into her duffel and picked it up before hustling back to the bathroom to grab the rolling suitcase. Tracy picked up the recycling bin stuffed full of supplies and grabbed the case of Slim Fast.

They headed out the front door of Wanda's apartment, back through the hallway that still smelled like a mix of rot and vomit, and out into the California sunshine.

Tracy stopped at the edge of the parking lot, fear and dread shocking her still. She turned to Wanda, the older woman's face paling as she stared at the empty parking spot in front of them.

The Suburban was gone.

CHAPTER TWENTY

MADISON

Sacramento, CA
2:00 p.m.

Brianna slowed as Madison pointed at the little brown bungalow two houses from the end of the street.

"It's so cute… and tiny!"

Madison smiled as she rolled her eyes. "My parents moved here when I left for college. They didn't want to take care of a big house anymore."

Peyton nudged her. "I like it. It's almost Lilliputian."

"It's like one of those tiny houses you see on TV." Tucker craned his head out the open window. "Does it come on wheels? I bet it's got wheels."

"Guys, come on. It's just a small house. This whole neighborhood was built in the forties. Haven't you seen any documentaries about the building after World War II?"

Each one of her friends gave her a blank look. "You know, the building and baby boom? All these tiny houses were built for the GIs just coming home from the war. Some people love these places."

Peyton half-coughed out a response. "Not six-foot-two guys."

"You're all just jealous." Madison pointed at the front step. "I bet none of you have a patio where you can grow tomatoes in March."

Brianna pulled the Jeep into the drive and turned off the engine. "I confess. Those patio tomatoes are making me green with envy."

"You mean green with hunger. I see one that's ripe right now." Tucker pushed open the passenger door and hopped out, walking over to the plants without another word.

"How can you be hungry? You ate half of that minimart!" Brianna shook her head. "Men."

"Watch it. There's still one of us in the car." Peyton poked Brianna in the shoulder with a grin a mile wide, but Madison wasn't interested. They'd been trying to get to her house for two days. She needed to find her family and hug them.

"Come on." Madison pushed open her door and Peyton and Brianna did the same. She walked past Tucker, who was crouched over the tomato plants and knocked on the front door. The sound carried through the dark house.

She shifted her weight back and forth, waiting. After thirty seconds, she knocked again, rapping her knuckles on the window instead of the wood. Still no answer.

Madison cursed under her breath and held her hands up to the glass, cupping her face to block out the afternoon sun. She couldn't make out much inside other than the familiar couch and now-worthless television.

"Brianna, check the garage, will you?" Madison shouted the question to her roommate while she made her way down the front porch to the side of the house. No evidence of anyone.

"No car in the garage." Brianna came around the corner shaking her head. "I don't think they're home."

"Where could they be? Why would they leave?" Madison frowned and rubbed at her forehead, trying to make sense of it. If her mom had received even one of her texts, then she'd be there, safe and sound, wouldn't she?

"So, I hate to be Captain Obvious, but do you have a key?" Tucker stood up, three ripe tomatoes in his hand. "'Cause it would be great to go inside out of the sun. My Nordic roots don't like the heat."

Madison dug in her pocket and fished out her keys before unlocking the front door. She pushed it open and popped her head inside. "Mom? Dad? Anyone home?"

No response.

With a disappointed exhale, she shoved the door wide and walked in, ushering her friends out of the sun and into the living room. It looked just like the last time she'd been home, apart from the lack of lights. Still the same brown leather sofa they'd had for a decade, the same TV and cabinet beneath it. Not a single picture on the wall had been bumped or moved.

If something bad happened to her parents, it wasn't

while they were home. She walked into the kitchen and stopped still. Someone had definitely gotten the message.

"Wow. Did your parents do all this?"

Madison stood gawking at the containers stuffed onto the counter. Every vase, Tupperware, water bottle, and trash can had been filled with water and squeezed onto the kitchen counter.

Madison nodded. "It must have been my mom. She got my texts." She glanced around in awe. "That's good, right? That means she prepared."

"Yeah, but where did she go?" Brianna picked up a piece of paper from the kitchen counter. "Looks like she inventoried the fridge and freezer, too."

Brianna held out the paper and Madison took it, scanning down the list of foods with dates next to each item, all in her mom's handwriting. "She went through all the perishable food and noted when to eat it. Some of it's listed today."

Madison shook her head. "She wouldn't have done that if she didn't think she'd be here."

"What if she left it for you or your dad?"

"Maybe." Madison set the list back down and walked over to the sink, resting her hands on it as she stared out into the backyard. "But something seems off. She wouldn't just disappear. If she'd planned to be gone for a while, she'd have left a note, eaten the food, something."

"Hey, Madison?" Peyton called out from down the hall. "You might want to see this."

Oh, no. Madison's chest constricted with dread. She

rushed into the guest bedroom where Peyton stood. "What is it?"

He pointed at the rumpled bed sheets. "Someone's been sleeping in that bed."

She frowned. "That's weird. My parents' bedroom is across the hall."

"That's not the only thing." Peyton walked past her and pushed open her parents' bedroom. "Look."

"Oh my goodness." Madison marveled at the stacks upon stacks of supplies. Gatorade and water. Toilet paper and paper towels. Protein powder and granola bars. "This is so my mom." Madison walked up to the cases of water and ran her fingers over the plastic. "She made me do Girl Scouts all the way through high school. I even had to earn the Gold Award."

Madison turned to Peyton. "She is all about being prepared."

"Not like Brianna's family, though right?" Peyton glanced around. "I mean, this is a good start, but unless there are some secret stairs to a bunker or fallout shelter, I'm not seeing a long-term survivalist here."

Madison shook her head. "No bunker. My mom isn't into doomsday stuff, more just everyday capabilities. But I can see her scrambling to get as much as she could if she thought something bad was about to happen."

"Maybe she's out foraging. She could be rounding up more supplies."

"It's a possibility, but I'd think she'd want to stay home and keep an eye over all of this. Especially if my dad's not here." Madison glanced around. "It doesn't look like he made it back yet."

"Where is he?"

Madison exhaled. "Anywhere from here to China. He had the San Francisco to Hong Kong flight yesterday."

"Ouch. That sucks."

Madison sat down on the edge of her mom's bed. "What about you? Aren't you worried about your dad?"

Peyton joined her on the edge of the mattress, his massive frame dipping the bed as he scooted back. "A little. But I shouldn't even give that jerk a second thought."

"Why not?"

"What good would it do? He basically disowned me, Madison. Kicked me out of the family and told me to not come back until I'd wised up." Peyton snorted. "I'd like to see the look on his face when he realizes all he's built is worthless."

Madison reached out and grabbed Peyton's hand. "I'm sorry. I know that's got to hurt. But he's still your dad. If you want to try and—"

"No." Peyton cut her off mid-sentence. He pulled his hand away from hers and stood up. "As far as I'm concerned, he's on his own."

"You mean that?"

Peyton threw out his hands. "Say I make it to Los Angeles. That somehow I can get a car and drive the four hundred miles all the way down there without gas or running into any kind of problems. Then what? I'm in freakin' Los Angeles. My dad was planning that massive party. I don't even know where he'd be. He could be at home, at the studio, the label, at some friend's mansion drinking champagne and swimming in the backyard pool like this is all one big vacation."

"And if he's not?"

Peyton stopped pacing. "Then he's got the pool out back, a kitchen full of food, and a gated front entrance. That should give him a little while, at least."

Madison hurt for her best friend. Not having a good relationship with her parents seemed impossible, but she knew lots of kids weren't so lucky. Even her own mom had a rough time growing up, but she hadn't shared many details. All Madison knew was that her mom hadn't spoken to her parents since before Madison was even born.

"I'm sorry, Peyton. People suck."

"My dad, especially." He sat back down with a sad smile on his face. "Enough about me. How are we going to find your parents?"

Madison thought it over. Part of her wanted to grab her pack and set off on foot, knocking on every door to ask about her mom. But another part of her said to stay put and wait. "I'm leaning toward the hug-a-tree approach."

"The what?"

"You know, if you're lost in the woods the best thing to do is sit down and hug a tree. It's what my parents taught me when we went backpacking. It's easier to find someone who's lost if they just stay put."

The more Madison thought it over, the more she settled on staying home. "My mom will come back. We just need to stay here and wait. Keep the place safe."

"And all these supplies." Peyton stood, up rubbing

his arms. "You think if we open the windows it'll warm up in here? I'm wondering how we're all going to stay warm tonight."

Madison shrugged. "It's worth a shot."

Peyton cranked open the window and a breeze shifted Madison's hair.

She glanced up in alarm. "Do you smell that?" She sniffed the air again. "It smells… like smoke."

CHAPTER TWENTY-ONE

MADISON

Sacramento, CA
3:00 p.m.

"What's going on?" Madison rushed out of the house, almost tripping over the step as she stumbled to a stop on the back patio. "Is something on fire?"

"Only Tucker's ego." Brianna nodded at the grill. "Seems he's not too manly, after all."

Tucker cast his girlfriend a glance. "I never said I was a grill master." He turned to Madison. "Please tell me you know how this works."

Madison sucked in a breath as her heartbeat slowed from hyperdrive to normal. "I thought you all had lit something on fire."

Tucker ducked his head. "Only my pride."

She laughed without hesitation for the first time in forever. "Lucky for you, I'm an expert griller. My mom's got a list of food and when to eat it in the kitchen. How about we crank this baby up and have us some steak?"

"If I didn't have a girlfriend…" Tucker's lame attempt at a joke was cut off by a tomato landing smack on his cheek. He caught it before it hit the ground. "Come on, babe, you know I was only joking."

"And you know I've got a mean fast pitch." Brianna brushed past Tucker and headed for the house. "If you don't get in here and help me pick, then you'll have to eat a veggie burger."

"Aw man, that's not fair." Tucker raced after her and the two disappeared into the house.

Madison turned back to the grill and pushed the ignition a few times before twisting the closest burner on. She might not know where her parents were, but she wasn't alone. She had three friends to share the afternoon, and they had food, water, and shelter. That was more than enough to be thankful for.

"You sure it's all right if we eat a bunch of food?" Peyton stopped beside her, a can of Coke in his hand. "My backpack's stuffed with food just like everyone else's. We don't have to eat what your parents have."

Madison cast him a look. "Don't be silly. Of course you can eat here. She waved at the kitchen. "All the meat in the fridge is probably bad and the stuff in the freezer is on the edge. If we don't cook it, we'll just have to get rid of it somehow." She glanced at the wheeled trash can supplied by the city. "I don't think trash pickup will happen this week."

Peyton sipped his soda but didn't say anything.

Whenever he grew silent, it meant he had more on his mind. "What is it?"

He looked up at the sky, focusing on the hints of color already appearing on the edge of dusk. "I know Brianna and Tucker are dead set on leaving, but what about you? What do you want to do?"

"Stay here. Wait for my parents. They'll come home. I know they will."

Peyton nodded, but didn't look at her. "If they do come back, where does that leave me?"

"What are you talking about?"

He swirled his half-empty can around and took another drink. "Will you still have room for me here? Or should I be prepared to leave?"

Madison turned to Peyton and reached for him, wrapping her arms around him in a sideways hug. His soda splashed as she pinned his arm to his side. How could he ever doubt his place in her home? She nuzzled his shirt. "It doesn't matter if we're down to our last Saltine, Peyton. You're basically family. Of course there's room for you here."

"*Eeewww.* You two need to get a room."

"Don't tell me there's kissing out there. You know I hate kissing."

Brianna and Tucker stopped in front of the grill, teasing smiles on both their faces.

"I thought we agreed to leave all the kissing to the two of you." Madison held out her hand and Brianna filled it with a plate of sliced-up zucchini and onions. Tucker held up two packages of chicken, both from the freezer. Just the sight of all the fresh food made

Madison's stomach clench. How long would it be before such a spread came this easy again?

Would anything like normalcy come back? Or was this the end of it, the last gasp of society fading into the dusk as the northern lights lit up the night?

She put the food on the grill and Tucker took the empty packages and plate back inside. The smell of cooking filled her nose and memories of a life too easy filled her mind. They had taken so much for granted. Not just electricity, but everything that went along with it: grocery stores, national farming corporations, the massive scale of modern food production.

The United States produced more food than every person inside its borders could ever hope to eat and many times over. Americans threw away so much food every day it was mind-boggling. She remembered the statistics from her sustainable farming class: 40 percent of all food grown in the US was thrown away. Enough to feed millions of people. Every. Single. Day.

How many people would wake up in a few days wishing they had canned all those strawberries and apples they had let rot in their fridges? How many would even know what to look for to see if food was still edible? Madison flipped over the chicken and veggies, thankful for what they had, but wary about the future.

Endless questions percolated in her head.

Peyton tapped her temple. "Whatcha thinking?"

Madison's brows knit together as she tried to put it into coherent words. "I'm worried. How long will it be before people figure out this is the best it's going to be?"

"What do you mean?"

Brianna perched on the edge of the patio table, leaning against the weathered wood. "It won't take long. Once people run out of food, they'll look to the government, the military. When they don't come…" She crossed her arms across her chest. "It'll get ugly fast."

"You really think everything's just stopped? That no one's going to try to help?"

"How can they? There's no power. How many police and military have reported to work? How many government employees actually showed up at their offices and tried to organize anything?"

Tucker came back outside, nodding along with his girlfriend. "Brianna's right. Everyone's always looking for someone else to tell them what to do. The police, military, members of state government, they all have bosses. Someone else in charge. When those people don't come up with a plan, everything will fall apart."

"I think you guys sell people short." Peyton scratched at his short hair. "Not everyone's a coward."

"It's not cowardice. It's self-preservation." Brianna pushed off the table, brown eyes bright with passion. "Besides, all those idiots we've elected lately, you really think they care about the little guy? You really think they're going to stick their necks out, risk their lives, to keep peace and order?"

She shook her head. "They only cared about one thing: power."

Peyton still wasn't ready to give in. "But don't they still have it? Aren't they still in charge?"

"In name only. All the power local, state, and federal officials have only exists because we allow it to exist.

What do you think will happen when the prisons fail? When the wardens don't show up to work? There's plenty of people out there who will jump into the void."

Brianna took a step closer. "All those bad guys out there won't stand around a wood-paneled room and spout a bunch of words about how we need to *do something*. They'll be out there taking control. By force." She swallowed. "By the time anyone in the government pulls up their big-boy pants and tries to help, it'll be too late."

Madison didn't know if Brianna was right, but she made some good points. Sitting back and waiting for help wouldn't do anything but waste time. She held up two plates stacked high with grilled veggies and meat. "I hope all that debating worked up your appetites."

Tucker grabbed a plate and set it on the table. "Just watching the two of them and I'm starving."

They all sat around the patio table, the mood lightening as they focused on dinner and not the uncertain future. Tucker loaded up his plate with a pile of zucchini and enough grilled chicken to feed a small football team.

Brianna chugged half a Gatorade and made a crack about burning off the calories with a late-night run. Even Peyton relaxed, eating and laughing until the crinkle of worry between his eyes smoothed away.

After they'd eaten every last scrap of food, the four of them leaned back, stuffed and satisfied. Living without electricity wasn't so bad if you got to do it with friends.

Madison hated to break the moment. She turned to

Brianna. "Please tell me you all are staying the night. I don't think you should be out on the roads when it's dark."

Brianna glanced at Tucker. "If it's all right, we'd love to. The Jeep's still got three-quarters of a tank, but I don't want to waste it. It'll take almost that much just to get to the cabin."

"That's with no detours."

Brianna nodded. "We'll need to keep an eye out for a way to get more."

Madison stood up and began collecting plates and her friends pitched in. "There's a bed in the guest room and a sleeper sofa in the living room." She paused. "And my parents' room, but…"

"If anyone sleeps there, it should be you."

Madison nodded, shoving her worry back down. "Thanks."

She took an armful of plates inside with Peyton and the others came along behind. As she set the dishes on the counter, a noise made her jump.

Bang. Bang. Bang.

Madison glanced up at Peyton in alarm. "What was that?"

He pointed toward the front door. "We've got a visitor."

CHAPTER TWENTY-TWO

TRACY

Sacramento, CA
6:00 p.m.

The case of Slim Fast wobbled on her hip. Tracy scanned the parking lot, checking for any sign of her Suburban. With every empty parking spot, panic rose inside her, growing from a tiny seed of fear and doubt to a full-fledged, heavy breathing, sweaty-palm catastrophe.

This can't be happening.

She turned to Wanda. "Did you see anyone? Hear anything?"

Wanda shook her head, the ashen pallor of her cheeks reminding Tracy of the remains of a campfire.

Barren.

Empty.

She swallowed down a wave of bile and tried to

think. They had spent all day clearing out Wanda's apartment. The Suburban could be hundreds of miles away by now.

"I can't believe… Why would anyone…" Wanda's thoughts trailed off, each one unfinished as if the refusal to utter the truth out loud would somehow make it less real.

Wanda took a hesitant step, arm outstretched to the parking spot where the Suburban sat an hour before. Tracy loved that SUV. It held a million people and twice as much gear. The transmission still worked with a hundred and five thousand miles. It even had a full tank of gas.

I risked getting shot for that gas.

A smell hung in the parking lot air, the pungent, thick combination of motor oil and rot. The more Tracy breathed in, the more it suffocated her, swallowing her up like a cloud of despair, pushing her closer to the brink of a breakdown. A crow cawed overhead, fat black body perched on the telephone line twenty feet away.

It would survive this apocalypse.

Carrion birds and cockroaches. They would make it. But what about a middle-aged librarian and her boss? Two women alone, without a car, fifteen miles from a house filled with supplies.

Wanda dropped her hand and closed her eyes, giving in to the fear that threatened to pull them both under. Tracy couldn't let it. She wasn't going to go down that road. She wasn't going to fail already.

She forced the truth between chapped lips.

"Someone stole it." *There. I said it.* Tracy inhaled through her nose and exhaled through her mouth, focusing on the act of breathing and ignoring the smell. She could control her breath. She could determine her own fate.

"But why?" Wanda's plaintive question did nothing to quell the anger rising inside of Tracy. Screw helplessness. She'd skipped through denial in record time. Anger was stage two and Tracy would be happy to spend the rest of the day mired in it.

All those self-help seminars, all the directing patrons to the grief section of the library. It only served to hone her focus now. *This is reality. This is the only thing that's real. Right here. This moment.*

Tracy inhaled and exhaled again, channeling her mind. "Because they needed to." She turned back toward Wanda's apartment. "We need to rest. Get a good night's sleep and start fresh in the morning."

"What are we going to do?"

Tracy closed her eyes. She couldn't do this now. "Let's just get back inside. We can figure it out in the morning."

Wanda opened her mouth to protest, but closed it just as fast. Her shoulders slumped as she trudged past Tracy and back toward her apartment.

Tracy didn't have the strength to tell Wanda her plan. Come morning, the woman would either be with her or be on her own. But first, she needed to tell her which car to steal.

* * *

SACRAMENTO, CA
8:00 a.m.

TRACY COULDN'T WAIT ANYMORE. SHE BARELY SLEPT the night before, tossing and turning on Wanda's couch as she thought and prayed about her daughter. If Madison made it home already and she wasn't there…

If she hadn't made it home and was trapped somewhere between Davis and the house or stuck on campus without power… Tracy could have driven herself mad thinking about all the what-ifs. Instead of thinking, she needed to be moving. Preferably on four wheels.

She slammed a cabinet in the kitchen. Waited. Slammed it again. At last, Wanda stumbled out of her bedroom, rubbing the sleep from her eyes.

"What's going on?"

Tracy threw the verbal grenade. "We need a car."

"I'm sorry, but I don't have one. That's why I was waiting for the bus." Wanda pushed her hair off her face and entered the kitchen, reaching for the coffee pot before she remembered the lack of power. She grabbed a bottle of water instead.

Tracy turned to face her, a grim determination setting her jaw. She had to make Wanda understand. "Who had the best vehicle here?"

Wanda blinked in slow-motion, pale eyelashes fanning up and down like the shutter on a vintage camera. At last she figured it out. "We can't steal a car!"

"Of course we can." Tracy walked over to the window, raising her hand to her brow to shield her sight from the early-morning sun, and scanned the parking lot. Most of the cars were tiny little things with gas tanks the size of her watering can back home. "We need something that runs well and has plenty of gas. An older model with pull up door locks and an accessible steering column. That or one where we can get the keys."

Wanda took a step back, bumping into the counter and sloshing her water. "We can't steal a car. Someone could need it. These people are my neighbors."

Tracy eyed her, expression unchanged. "Then pick a dead one. Dead people don't need transportation."

"You're serious."

"How else do you think we're going to get home?" She pointed at the supplies they'd hauled back inside the night before. "We can't walk fifteen miles carrying this stuff under our arms. It'll take us days."

Wanda's brow knitted as she thought it over. "So we'll be slow. That's okay. We can take a while."

Tracy raised an eyebrow. "And what will we do at night?"

Wanda hesitated. "It's bright at night. We can find somewhere to rest, sleep in shifts."

"We'll be robbed before we make it two miles. Maybe worse."

"You don't know that."

Tracy pointed at first herself and then Wanda. "Look at us. We're a pair of middle-aged women with nothing more than a World War II pistol between us. It probably won't even fire. What would we do if someone accosted us?"

Wanda glanced over at the bags she'd packed. "We don't really need any of this stuff. We could do without."

"What if they want more than food?"

"That wouldn't happen."

"Are you sure?"

Wanda didn't answer. Instead, she turned to look out at the management building. She walked over to the sliding glass door and yanked it open. After standing and listening for a moment, she glanced back at Tracy. "Do you hear that?"

"Hear what?"

"It's too quiet. I think the generators shut off last night." She shut the door and came back into the kitchen. Her hands trembled as she spoke. "Without the generators, there's no way to keep the residents on oxygen alive. Or keep any food cold. Or run the HVAC to the main building." She glanced down at the linoleum, teeth sneaking out to nibble her lower lip. "You really think we'll be robbed if we walk?"

Tracy nodded.

Wanda stood in the kitchen staring at the floor for so long, Tracy thought she'd fallen asleep standing up. At last, she nodded. "Okay." She looked up, fear and determination warring on her face. "I have an idea."

After eating a quick breakfast and getting dressed, Wanda led Tracy out of the front door and around the edge of her building. They headed down a set of stairs running alongside the faded yellow stucco and emerged in a smaller parking lot tucked between the back gate of the community and Wanda's building.

She slowed to a stop and leaned close to Tracy, her voice dropping to a whisper. "See that little gray car across the lot?"

Tracy squinted. "The Nissan Leaf?"

Wanda nodded. "The man who lives below me owns it, but he can't drive. He was one of the residents on 24/7 oxygen. His daughter bought the car so that she'd have something to get around in when she flew down from Seattle to visit."

"Do you think it has gas?"

Wanda bobbed her head again. "Always. He keeps it filled up. And it's part electric, so the mileage is great."

Tracy hesitated. Would it even work now? Did the CME do anything to hybrid cars? She didn't really know. "Are there any other options? Something older and not electric?"

Wanda chewed on her lip. "I've got an upstairs neighbor that drives an old Impala, but that thing's always in the shop."

Tracy exhaled. She didn't want to break down on the road. "All right. Nissan Leaf it is. Can we get the keys?"

Wanda nodded. "Should be able to. George always leaves his screen door open."

"Just like some other people I know."

A blush crept up Wanda's neck. "He's the one who gave me the idea. But we'll need to be careful. He has a cat."

Great. All they had to do was break into a stranger's apartment, hope they weren't attacked by a house cat, and pray the car turned on when they got inside. She adjusted the butt of Wanda's revolver that she'd tucked into the back of her jeans.

It might not fire, but it was better than nothing. She nodded at the apartment. "Let's go."

Wanda took the lead, creeping toward the man's patio as she scanned the lot for any movement. Tracy hoped the management guy from earlier didn't catch them, or anyone else for that matter. If the police didn't care enough to come save the people dying in the complex, then they probably wouldn't care about a car theft, but she didn't know for sure.

Getting trapped in jail when the world was falling apart wasn't part of her plan.

Wanda motioned at a little patio with a bistro set and a dead plant. "It's this one." She eased over the half-height wall, her short, stocky legs barely clearing the top.

Tracy followed behind. "Are you sure he's not home?"

Wanda shrugged. "I'm not sure of anything anymore." She gave the screen door a yank and it slid open. The glass door yielded just as easy. As soon as it cracked an inch, the smell hit them, followed by a plaintive yowling.

Oh, no. Tracy braced herself, pulling her sleeve down over her hand and smothering her nose with the fabric to cut down on the putrid odor.

They eased inside, stopping a foot into the room as their eyes adjusted to the dim light.

George hadn't left home. His dead body lay just as he'd lived, sitting in his recliner, facing the TV, one hand dangling off the side with a remote beneath it on the floor.

His face had turned gray and ashen, his eyes clouded and milky blue.

Tracy took another step when a little orange fluff ball darted out from the hall, howling and yowling at her feet.

Wanda bent down to pet it. "Hey Fireball, how are you?" She scooped up the scrap of a cat and it nuzzled her cheek before licking her nose. She smiled at Tracy. "Whenever George had a hospital stay, I'd watch this little guy." She glanced at George's decomposing body. "Guess I won't be doing that anymore."

Tracy turned away from the recliner. "How long has he been gone, do you think?"

"Looks like a few days." Wanda rubbed the scruff behind Fireball's neck. "This guy's been on his own too long. I'm surprised he didn't start nibbling."

Tracy fought back a wave of nausea. Fireball wouldn't be the only animal trapped in a house and starving. If they hadn't come inside, it wouldn't have been long before he turned to his master to keep himself alive. In a way, humans weren't any different. She was a scavenger now, too.

She motioned toward the kitchen. "Can you grab the cat food? We'll take Fireball with us. No sense in leaving him here to starve. Where are the keys?"

"They should be in the hall."

Tracy took a step that way when a voice stopped her still.

"*Hey, I found an open one. Come on!*"

Shit. She turned to Wanda. "Run!"

CHAPTER TWENTY-THREE

TRACY

SACRAMENTO, CA
9:30 a.m.

"CHRIST, MAN, YOU SMELL THAT? THIS ONE'S RIPE."

"Don't be a little bitch. Just tell me if there's anything worth stealing. And hurry up. That asshole from maintenance will be making his rounds any minute."

No no no. Tracy ran down the hall with Wanda scurrying to catch up behind her. They had to hide, and fast. Whoever was breaking in didn't sound like anyone they wanted to know. If they got caught inside this apartment, who knows what would happen.

The sound of the sliding glass door opening shot a bolt of panic down her spine. She'd never make it to the front door in time. Tracy scanned the hall, tugging open the first door she could reach. A coat closet. It would have to do.

She rushed into it, shoving old coats and a vacuum out of the way as Wanda rushed in behind her. Tracy tugged the door shut just as a flashlight beam lit up the hall. Had they been spotted? Did the guy breaking in see them?

She held her breath as the light bounced around before receding.

"Man, this guy went out the right way, sittin' in front of the boob tube, empty can of PBR on the side table. We should all be this lucky."

"Come on Hank, let's just get what we need and get out. The smell's makin' me sick."

"Oh, is little Ricky squeamish?"

"Shut up, asshole."

"What you want to bet this guy didn't even know what hit him? Look at that oxygen tube. It probably shut off and he croaked, just like that."

"Who cares? His loss is our gain. You search the kitchen. I'm hitting up the bathroom. Bet this guy had all sort of meds."

Tracy managed to suck in a breath of air. They hadn't been spotted. If they could just stay still and quiet…

A brush of fur tickled her nose. *Oh, no.* She turned to see Fireball climbing up Wanda's shoulder and into her hair. She practically hissed. "You brought the cat?"

"Of course!" Wanda whispered back. "You think I'm going to let those guys hurt him?"

Tracy steeled herself. There was no way they'd make

it out of there without being found now. Wanda might as well have put a giant flashing beacon in the hall. She could see it now, a big banner with Hollywood lights: "Hey bad guys, two crazy ladies and a cat are hiding right here!"

She whispered again. "Do you know them?"

Wanda shook her head as Fireball climbed down her other shoulder and batted at the fringe of a scarf hanging on a hook.

Great. Tracy tried to stay calm. The more in control she could be, the better shot they had of making it out alive. She fingered the butt of the pistol sticking out the back of her jeans. Worse came to worst, she could use it. Tracy knew how to fire a gun. She'd hunted as a kid, shot a handgun for target practice, even went shooting with Walter and Madison as part of a 4-H camping trip when her daughter was twelve.

But shooting a person was a million times different than shooting a painted circle on a bale of hay or even a deer at the end of a rifle sight.

Her palms grew sweaty and Tracy wiped them on the front of her jeans. She needed a steady grip, not a slick one.

The sound of metal jingling made Tracy's teeth clench.

One of the men shouted from the kitchen. "You think this stiff's got a ride?"

"A guy who breathes from a tank all day? Naw, man, he can't drive."

"Then what's with these keys?"

Damn it. They'd found the car keys in the kitchen,

not in the hall. She hadn't even been close. Tracy needed those keys. She had to get home to her supplies and to her family. What if Walter had made it home and she wasn't there? What if he'd shown up and found the house empty?

Would he think the worst? Would he come looking for her? She needed to get out of this apartment, get home, and be safe. They couldn't take her best shot to get there.

Tracy eased the gun from out of her waistband and pulled back the hammer.

"What are you doing?" Wanda whispered as the cat squirmed in her grip.

"Getting ready. They can't take the car."

"You can't shoot them!" Wanda's voice edged up a notch and Tracy hissed at her to be quiet.

The cat let out a little yowl.

"You hear that?"

"What?"

"Sounded like a damn cat."

"Ignore it. Little bastard's gonna be dead in a few days anyway."

"I hate cats. Damn things were always crapping in my front yard."

Tracy braced herself.

"I said let it go, man. We ain't got time for your shit."

The cat squirmed again and Wanda lost her grip. It landed on the crowded floor of the closest with a thud. Tracy inhaled and brought her other hand up to grip the revolver. She held the gun down and out in front of her, arms straight, barrel pointed toward the floor.

Fireball meowed and pawed at the door. It was only a matter of time, now. Footsteps sounded in the hall. *Thud. Thud. Thud.* The flashlight beam swept the bottom of the closet and Fireball reached out to swat at it, his little paw dipping below the door to stretch out into the hall beyond.

Wanda reached to pull the cat back, but Tracy shook her head. It was too late. No sense in waiting. She reached for the door handle and twisted, popping the door free before she pulled back and kicked. Her boot hit the door a few inches to the left of the handle and it flew open.

From the sound of the smack and garbled curse, she'd found her target. Tracy eased into the hall, gun raised, arms straight. A man stood half behind the door, half not, hands covering his face.

Blood oozed between his fingers. He unleashed a string of vulgar curses, his mouth obviously unharmed.

"Stay back!" Tracy shouted at him and the man finally looked up, somehow surprised by her presence.

"Hey now! Easy!" He held his bloody hands up in the air. From her vantage point, most of his face was in shadow, the dropped flashlight casting an eerie, almost hallucinatory glow around his feet. He had to be over six feet tall, with broad shoulders and a stance that said he packed more muscle than the average office worker.

Tracy would be no match for him without the gun. She motioned with it. "Step back!"

He licked at a trail of blood that seeped into his

mouth, but didn't move. "Listen lady. You already broke my nose. What are you gonna do now, shoot me?"

"If I have to. I said, step back."

"And if I don't?"

She cocked her head. "I know how to use this. Don't think I won't."

While Tracy trained the gun on the man, Wanda slipped out into the hall, the damn cat back in her arms. "Let the cat go, Wanda. He's caused enough problems."

"Hey, Wanda! Is that you?"

She stammered a response. "W-who's a-as-sking?"

"It's Richard from maintenance. Remember me? I helped you with your HVAC."

She sniffed back some snot. "You don't look familiar."

"Come on, you know me. Tell your friend here to put down the gun and we can all talk, like civilized folk."

Wanda glanced at Tracy and shook her head.

"I'm not lowering the gun. Now do what I said and step back."

"Hey what the hell's going on out—" The man from the kitchen appeared, his hands full with a bag of Cheetos and a six-pack of beer. "Whoa! Hey now!"

"Hold up your hands!"

He complied, hands and snacks up in the air before Tracy had to tell him twice. "Now set the beer down and toss me the keys you found. Nice and easy."

The man from the kitchen didn't move. Instead, he opened his mouth. "How about we talk about this? I bet we can come to a solution."

Tracy inhaled. They weren't going to give up the

keys. Not without a fight. She could tell by the way the one with the broken nose kept eyeing Wanda and how the one from the kitchen wouldn't put down the beer. They thought they had the upper hand even though she had the gun.

She didn't want to shoot anyone, but she needed the keys. Tracy pointed the gun at the guy with the broken nose as she addressed the one from the kitchen. "Give me the keys or I shoot him in the leg."

"Hank, listen to the lady." He wiped at the blood on his face and turned to his friend, nerves finally breaking through his bravado. "We don't need the car. We've already got one. Throw her the keys, man."

"She's bluffing."

"I'm not." Tracy bent her knees slightly, easing into position in case she needed to shoot. *Pretend it's target practice. Pretend it's not real.* She could do this. She could protect herself. "I'll count to three. One."

"Shit! Hank, come on!" The man with the broken nose slammed his hand on the hallway wall to get his partner's attention, but it wasn't Hank who reacted.

Fireball yowled and launched from Wanda's arms, a flying ball of fur and claws. Wanda shouted and lunged for him. "Fireball, no!"

Everything slowed. Tracy had been in a few life-and-death situations before, many years ago. Her childhood hadn't been a walk in the park. But it had been different then. She hadn't had a husband and a daughter depending on her. It'd been just her and her stuffed rabbit and just enough room to hide under the bed.

She'd been too young to do anything but hide then.

But now she was all grown up. Strong. Capable. Dependable. She sucked in a breath.

It was as if the air turned to gelatin, every movement pushing against the semi-solid substance, slowing time down to almost a stop. Wanda's arms reached out, stretching for the cat as it darted between the man's legs.

He dove for Wanda, seeing his chance to gain the upper hand. His fingers clawed at Wanda's hair, tangling in the strands. He planned to break her neck. Tracy saw it all like a still from a movie. The minuscule movements, the intent on his face writ plain.

Tracy steadied her arms, found the sight, and pulled the trigger.

Boom!

The sound echoed through the apartment as the recoil shoved her arms up in the air. A puff of smoke and the smell of cordite overpowered the stench of death in the apartment.

The man's mouth fell open.

He gaped at her, head bending down to look at the hole she'd blasted straight into the left side of his chest.

Hank, the man from the kitchen, shouted and threw the beer on the ground before charging toward her. If he'd only turned and run.

Tracy didn't hesitate. The trigger compressed, the revolver fired. Another shot, another hit.

Hank swung back, the first round hitting his shoulder. He kept coming like the Terminator, relentless and undeterred. Tracy fired again.

Blood and carnage bloomed on his chest. Hank fell

to his knees, hands reaching up to hold the wound. It didn't help. In moments, he fell to the floor, three feet from his partner, face down in the other man's blood.

Ringing. It's all Tracy could hear. A deafening ringing. She blinked. Had it been an hour or mere seconds? She couldn't be sure.

She turned to Wanda. The woman cowered on the floor, hands over her head like a child trying in vain to disappear. "Are you all right?" Tracy couldn't tell if she'd spoken out loud.

She opened her mouth to try again when Wanda moved, peeling her arms away to glance up through wet lashes. "You shot them!"

"I had to."

A tear hit Wanda's cheek. "What the hell do we do now?"

Not fall apart, that's what.

Tracy shoved down the rising fear and vomit that threatened to drown her. There was plenty of time to grieve and process. Right now they needed to move. She held out her hand. "We get the keys and we run."

CHAPTER TWENTY-FOUR

MADISON

SACRAMENTO, CA
   8:00 p.m.

"WHO COULD BE KNOCKING?" MADISON STARED AT
the front door, the sound of her blood whooshing
through her veins so loud she could barely think.

"It's probably just a neighbor." Peyton shrugged like
nothing was the matter. "Just answer it."

Madison didn't think any neighbor of her parents'
would be knocking at this time of night. She glanced at
her watch. It was after eight. Granted, the sky didn't
exactly scream middle of the night, what with it lit up in
an arcing field of color, but still.

Nothing good could come from a late-night visit.
She exhaled and walked to the door. "Can I help you?"
She shouted through the wood, unwilling to just throw
it open.

"It's William Donovan from a few doors down. Is everything all right?"

Madison rose up on her toes to stare through the peep hole. A man in his fifties stood on the other side, hands stuffed in his jean pockets. He didn't look all that threatening, but her parents had never mentioned him and Madison didn't remember him from her visits home this past year.

She unlocked the door with caution, barely opening it wide enough to stick her head through. "Hi. Is there something I can do for you? It's getting late."

He eyed her up and down, at least what he could see, and Madison fought the urge to slam the door in his face.

"Where's Tracy?"

"She's busy. I'm her daughter, Madison. Can I help you?"

The man shifted on his feet and he glanced at the Jeep in the driveway. They should have parked it in the garage. He pulled one hand out of a pocket and wiped at the corners of his mouth. "Your dad here?"

"Not at the moment." If the man was a neighbor, he had to know her dad flew for a living. She couldn't lie about everything.

"You doin' all right?"

This was getting them nowhere and Madison had almost had enough. "I'm fine. It's getting late. Is there something I can help you with?"

"Like I said, I'm William Donovan, but you can call me Bill. Just wanted to check and see if you all were okay. I saw that Jeep parked in the drive and hadn't seen your mother come back, so I was worried."

Madison scrunched up her brows. "What do you mean, you saw my mother leave?"

A smirk threatened the corners of his lips. "She left pretty early this morning with another woman. Haven't seen them come back and that garage looks pretty empty. Wanted to make sure there wasn't anything bad going on, you know."

Madison tried to mask her relief. Her mother had been home that morning. It had to mean she was okay. Safe. Maybe she was just out getting supplies or helping a friend. She'd be back. Soon.

Bill was just a concerned neighbor, looking out for her. Madison smiled. "I came home from college this morning. With all the power out, we can't exactly have class."

He whistled and leaned back to catch a glimpse of the driveway. "So that Jeep there is yours? Pretty fancy for a college kid. Looks like it could handle some serious off-roading."

Madison's friendly smile faded. It was one thing to check and make sure the house wasn't being robbed, but poking around about the Jeep didn't seem neighborly. Just the opposite, in fact. She tried to keep calm. "I wouldn't know. I've only ever taken it on the streets."

Bill nodded, but didn't make a move to leave. "You, um… here all alone?"

Shit. The last thing she wanted to do was tell him the truth. Who knew what he was after. Food? Weapons?

Just assessing the neighborhood for threats? Madison tried to dodge. "It's getting late. Thanks for stopping by to check on the place. I'll let my mom know you came by."

Bill still didn't get the hint. He scratched at the back of his head. "We missed your parents at the neighborhood meeting this afternoon."

Madison frowned. "What meeting?"

"We all got together at Penny's place and talked about the state of affairs."

"Why weren't we invited?"

"Didn't think anyone was home."

Madison exhaled. What was he getting at? She tried to fish for some more information. Feigning ignorance could come in handy. "Has anyone heard anything? Is there a timeline for when the power's coming back on?"

Bill shrugged. "I heard it isn't coming back on. That grids all over are fried."

Madison pretended to be shocked. "That can't be true."

"You know Bob down the street?" He pointed north.

Madison shook her head.

"He works for the power company. Says there's nothing they can do. No one has any backup transformers, and even if they did, the grid's in such bad shape nothing will work. Around here, we rely on natural gas to generate electricity. Without the grid up and running, the gas can't get converted. We're SOL."

Madison voiced a thought she'd been bouncing around for a while. "What about over the ridge? There's all those wind turbines on the hills next to the highway. There have to be hundreds on the way to the Bay Area."

"Not our grid. Maybe the Bay Area could get power going again if the wires going to the turbines aren't shot." Bill shrugged. "But that won't help us."

"What does everyone here want to do?"

"Hang tight, mostly." He almost snorted. "Some of these idiots actually think help is coming."

"You don't?"

He paused long enough for Madison to get the creeps. "Help isn't coming. You know that as well as I do."

"I don't know anything."

He nodded at the Jeep. "So all those supplies in the back are what, accidental?"

Madison swallowed.

"We're all screwed. No power. No police. No military. Nothing but our wits and our strength."

"What are you saying?"

Bill stepped closer and Madison fought the urge to step back. He couldn't see inside with the way she held the door and Madison wanted it to stay that way. "I'm saying, it's survival of the fittest now."

Madison ran her tongue across her lips. It scraped like sandpaper across wood. "I think you're selling people short."

"Am I? You really think everything is going to be fine?"

"I didn't say that."

"Then what are you saying, exactly? Because based on what you've got stashed away in your car, I bet you've got a hell of a lot more tucked away inside that house. I saw Tracy pull that Suburban in late the other night. It looked stuffed to the gills." He wiped at his face. "When things get hard, are you all planning on sharing the wealth?"

Madison exhaled. She didn't know what to do. Part of her wanted to say of course they'd share, but was that true? When it came down to her friends and family or a neighbor she'd never met, who mattered more?

Where did her allegiances lie? In her heart, Madison knew the answer, but she hated to admit it. This man wasn't any different from her. She'd already run from the police and stepped over a dead body to steal food. How much lower would she go? Would she have any morals left when it came to survival?

Had she changed so much in such a short time?

Her grip on the door wobbled. "I don't think I want to have this discussion anymore. Have a good night, Mr. Donovan." Madison moved to shut the door, but the man stepped forward in a rush, slamming a thick, meaty hand on the wood.

"I don't think we're done here."

Before Madison could react, the door swung wide. Peyton gripped the door handle in one hand and her father's old baseball bat in the other. The metal shaft shined in the light. "If Madison says you're done, then you're done."

Her parents' neighbor might have been larger than Madison, but he was nothing compared to Peyton. With a flex of his arm, Peyton made his intentions clear. He wasn't to be messed with, and neither was Madison.

After a moment, the neighbor stepped back with a nod. "All right." He held up his hands. "I don't want any trouble." He turned to Madison. "You tell your mom there's another meeting tomorrow at noon. The Palmers' place. If she makes it back, we'd love to have her."

"If she doesn't, I'll be attending for her."

Bill shot her a glance, but said nothing, opting instead to back off the front porch. He took one more look at the Jeep, lingering for a beat in the drive, before walking to the street and turning south. They watched him until he disappeared around the first corner.

Madison exhaled and leaned against the wall as Peyton shut the door. "Thanks for the help."

Peyton lifted the bat and rested it on his shoulder. "No problem. I've always wanted to be the heavy, anyway."

"Where'd you find that?"

He shrugged. "The garage. It was a little dusty, but a couple swings took care of that." Peyton patted the bat with a grin. "I figured better to show we mean business but not tip our hand."

"You mean the guns?"

"Exactly." Peyton's smile faded. "After that little performance, we can't let our guard down. Not for a minute."

Madison frowned. She didn't want to think the worst of her parents' neighbors, but the visit unnerved her. "What do you think he was after?"

Peyton swung the bat around in a slow arc before answering. "Everything we have, I'd guess."

She hoped he was wrong, but the more Madison thought about the visit, the more she agreed with Peyton. She pushed off the wall and pointed toward the kitchen. "Come on, let's get Brianna's Jeep in the garage and hash out a plan."

DAY THREE

CHAPTER TWENTY-FIVE

MADISON

Sacramento, CA
11:30 a.m.

"I don't think it's necessary. What if someone sees it? What if you need it while I'm gone?"

Brianna slid the unloaded handgun across the kitchen table. "The meeting could just be a ruse to draw you out."

Madison shook her head. She wasn't walking into a meeting with a bunch of confused and worried neighbors with a gun shoved inside the waistband of her jeans. She pushed it back across the table. "No. I'm not taking it."

Brianna scowled, but said nothing. The handgun sat between them, a visual reminder of their differing opinions.

"What's going on?" Peyton walked into the kitchen,

201

pausing as he noticed the gun. "Staring at that thing isn't going to conjure up more ammunition, although it'd be a neat trick if it worked."

Madison cast him a glance. "Brianna wants me to take it to the meeting. I said no."

Peyton let out a whistle. "What do you think, Tucker?"

Brianna's boyfriend scratched at the back of his neck. "I don't know. They both have a point. Madison thinks if someone sees it, it could cause a scene. And if that jerk from yesterday is planning on breaking in, we might need it here."

"We do have the shotgun." Peyton nodded at the handgun. "That thing has, what? Ten rounds? It won't do as much good as the box full of shells."

"Ten is better than none." Madison leaned back in the chair as she crossed her arms over her chest. "Besides, just pointing it at someone could get the point across. You saw how Bill reacted when you showed up with the bat."

Peyton shrugged. "What if he's armed this time?"

"I don't know if anyone in this neighborhood has a gun. You saw how hard it was to purchase a firearm here. I wouldn't be surprised if we were the only house on the block with any kind of weapon."

Tucker spoke up. "Haven't you seen that YouTube guy who makes weapons out of anything? He made an air gun out of a Coke can and a spear or something out of a garden hose. This whole 'hood could be weaponized."

"Too bad YouTube doesn't exist anymore." Brianna

huffed her displeasure. "I could go for a few more defenses, myself."

Madison reached for her roommate's hand and gave it a squeeze. Her chipped nail polish reminded Madison of how much things had changed in such a short time. A manicure seemed so ridiculous when the talk of basic defense and survival was on the agenda.

"You don't have to stay. If you and Tucker want to get out of here and head for Truckee, do it."

Brianna pulled her hand away. "And leave you in danger? No way. I'm not leaving until I know you're safe."

"Same here." Tucker eased his hands in his jean pockets. "We're staying until either your parents make it home or we know more." He glanced at his girlfriend. "If it turns out you're on your own…"

Brianna filled in the rest. "Then you're coming with us. The cabin's got more than enough room for you and Peyton, too."

Madison swallowed down a wave of emotion. Her mom had to be all right. Madison had stayed up most of the night waiting for her, hoping she'd hear the familiar rumble of the Suburban pull into the drive. But the sound never came and in the morning, her mom still wasn't home.

She couldn't even think about her dad. He could be anywhere. If he was still alive. If he'd been in the air when the CME hit, he'd have been cut off from all communication. Her dad was a good pilot, but could he land a 747 with only his eyes as a guide? Over water?

With a deep breath, Madison pushed the fears aside.

Right now she needed to focus on keeping everyone here safe, their supplies secret and secure, and finding out what the neighbors knew. They were in the capital of California; someone who lived in the neighborhood had to have more information.

The chair squeaked cross the tile as she stood up. "It's almost noon. I'm heading over."

"I'll come with you." Peyton took a step toward her, but Madison waved him off. "No. They need to know the house isn't empty. Bill didn't see Brianna or Tucker, remember? For all he knows it's just the two of us. Let's keep him in the dark as long as possible."

She paused, taking a moment to make eye contact with each of her friends. "If anything happens, do what you have to do to survive."

Brianna nodded as she stood up. She eased around the table and gave Madison a hug, a curl tickling Madison's nose. "Be safe, okay? I want you back here ASAP and in one piece, all right?"

Madison nodded and Brianna let her go.

"Don't worry about us, we'll be okay." Peyton gave her a pat on the shoulder, his eyes full of emotion.

Tucker managed a nod. "We're good. Just concentrate on finding out as much as you can. If there's any word on the solar weather, I'd love to know."

"Will do. Thanks, guys." Madison exhaled a shaky breath before turning toward the living room.

Without a single look back, Madison tugged open the front door and stepped outside. She made a show of locking it behind her before stepping down off the front porch and walking toward the street.

The Palmers were an older couple Madison had met a few times while home on break. They lived five houses down and across the street in a little Cape Cod about the same size as her parents' house. All the houses in the neighborhood were built in the forties, one of the first modern-planned tract housing developments in the area.

Over the years, a few of the houses had been expanded or topped and turned into little castles, but both her parents' house and the Palmers' stayed true to their roots. A pair of women she didn't know were walking on the sidewalk across the street, headed in the same direction. Madison smiled as she crossed the street toward them.

"Are you going to the neighborhood meeting?"

The woman closest to her smiled and nodded. With dark brown hair and freckles across her nose, she couldn't have been older than thirty. She held out her hand. "I'm Anna, this is Brooke. We live off Verde Villa."

Madison shook both of their hands before pointing back the way she came. "I'm Madison. Tracy and Walt's daughter. We live just—"

"I know Tracy." Brooke held out her hand and Madison shook it, too. "She's been helping me with beginning reader books for my daughter. It's so nice to have a librarian in the neighborhood."

Madison smiled and fell into step beside them as the three of them walked up to the Palmers' house. "Were you all able to come yesterday?"

Anna nodded. "I came. Brooke was busy with her

little ones. I didn't see your mom or dad. Are they home?"

Madison hesitated. "Not right now, but we didn't want to miss anything."

Neither woman said anything, but the glance between them spoke volumes. Madison wanted to tell them not to worry, that as a college student she was a lot more prepared than they were to handle the future. But she didn't.

They had arrived.

The front door to the home opened and Mrs. Palmer beamed. "Madison! So good to see you. We were wondering if you would make it home all right. Anna, Brooke." Mrs. Palmer craned her neck, looking for anyone else. "Is your mom not coming?"

"Not today." Madison eased inside and Mrs. Palmer shut the door.

"You give her my best, will you? I've been meaning to tell her that canning book she found for me at the library might turn out to be a godsend."

Madison smiled in response. She hoped she'd get the chance to tell her mom so many things. As she walked into the living room, Madison tried to get her bearings. About twenty neighbors stood around the room, clustered into groups of three or four. She thought about the layout of the neighborhood and how many people might have been invited.

There had to be over a hundred little houses in the subdivision. Where was everyone else? Since her parents hadn't moved in until Madison was already in college, she didn't know many people. Apart from Mrs. Palmer and the two women she'd just met, Madison couldn't place a single face. She wished her mom was there by her side.

She would know who could be trusted and who to look out for, who to sidestep and who to befriend. If the power stayed out for as long as she feared it might, these people could be the difference between survival and death.

With a deep breath, Madison walked toward the closest group of people, straining to hear their conversation before she butted in.

A man with gray hair pushed a set of bifocals up his nose as he gesticulated at the street, already mid-sentence. "—have to be coming, don't they? Isn't this what FEMA's for?"

The woman across from him nodded. "The Red Cross, too. They should be here already. When it flooded, the fire department came right away and the Red Cross set up a trailer at the end of the block."

They wouldn't be much help. Madison smiled and eased past them, hoping someone would have some information she could use. Another cluster of people huddled around the fireplace as if they would somehow draw comfort from a cold and empty grate.

"I haven't heard from Monica since the power went out." The woman speaking tugged a purple knit cardigan closer around her. "She works at the Med Center downtown."

Madison perked up and stepped close enough to become part of the conversation. "I'm sorry, but is that the UC Davis Medical Center?" Madison smiled an apology and continued. "I go to school at Davis. My mom's Tracy Sloane."

"Oh, you're Madison!" The woman smiled. "Tracy has said so much about you. You're studying to be a farmer, right?"

Madison gave a sheepish smile. "Sort-of. My mom couldn't make the meeting so I came instead, but I'm not home much, so I don't know anyone here."

The woman held out her hand. "I'm Tabitha." She nudged the man to her right. "My husband Richard and I live just down the street. The little blue bungalow with the orange door."

Madison nodded. She knew the one. "Nice to meet you." She shook first Tabitha's hand and then Richard's.

"And this is Jean, she's our next-door neighbor."

Jean, an older woman with blonde hair and bright red eyeglasses held out her hand. "Your mom and I started a book club a few months ago." She glanced at the dark TV. "It might get a whole lot more popular if the televisions don't come back on."

Madison let out a little laugh. Everyone she had met so far was nice. Normal. Nothing like that Bill guy who gave her the creeps the night before. She exhaled before testing the waters. "Have any of you heard anything? It's been a long time to be without power."

Everyone in the little circle shook their head. "Usually we know something by now, but I haven't heard a thing." Tabitha glanced at her husband. "Like I was saying, Monica Fillers lives on the other side of us and she's a nurse at the Med Center. She hasn't been home since the power went out. We haven't ventured outside the neighborhood, but Bill from the street over did. He said the power's out everywhere."

Jean crinkled her nose. "I worry about all the sick people in hospitals and all the poor nurses and doctors tending to them."

Tabitha nodded. "What about the police? How can they cope without radios?"

"I worry more about the prisons." Richard frowned. "Folsom's not that far from here. What if they don't have power? How long can it stay secure?"

Madison had all the same concerns. "I drove home from Davis. The power's out there, too. I think it's out everywhere."

Jean's mouth fell open. "What do you mean, everywhere?"

Madison blinked. Did these people really not know? Did they think it was an isolated incident and everything would just be repaired if they waited it out? She didn't know what to say. How much information should she give them? The last thing she wanted was to start a panic. That wouldn't help anyone.

She opened her mouth to say something when another voice called out. "I think everyone who's coming is here. Let's get this meeting started."

Madison turned in time to see Bill, the man from the night before, take up position in the front of the room. Madison exhaled. *At least he's not breaking into our house.*

Yet.

CHAPTER TWENTY-SIX

TRACY

SACRAMENTO, CA
  12:00 p.m.

THE SMELL OF FRESH BLOOD MIXED WITH THE STINK of decay, and Tracy fought to swallow the rising swell of saliva in the back of her mouth. She couldn't vomit. Not over what she'd done.

The horror of it would come later; she knew this much. That night under the bed she'd been eerily calm, too. Just like this.

But later…

Oh, later had been almost worse than the experience itself. So many nightmares. So many screams jolting her out of the relative safety of a foster bed. Tracy swallowed again and bent over the man from the kitchen. *Hank.*

She reached for his arm, plucking it off the ground with a pincher grip on his threadbare flannel. A jingle of metal on metal rewarded her efforts. Tracy scooped up the keys as the widening pool of blood encroached on the now-empty space. She dropped Hank's arm.

It squished as it fell, the sticky plop a reminder of the finality of her actions.

Tracy straightened up. "I've got the keys. Let's get back to your place, grab the supplies, and get out of here."

Wanda leaned against the counter, one arm propping her up like a tent pole at the big top. "I don't think I can do this." Her cheeks flamed, two bright spots on an otherwise ashen face.

"Yes you can."

Wanda's cheeks sucked in and bulged out, the precursor to what came next. The vomit landed on the linoleum, splashing over Ricky or Richard, whatever his name had been. The man who started it all. Wanda clutched at her belly, heaving until Tracy was sure the blood vessels in her eyes would burst.

At last, she righted herself, wiping her mouth with the back of her hand. "I'm sorry."

"Don't be. Just get ready. We've got to go."

Tracy led the way out of the apartment, past George still lounging in the recliner, his blind eyes oblivious to the violence behind him. Wanda followed a few steps behind, clearing her throat as she went. The sun hit Tracy's face and she almost hissed.

Too bright. Too real.

She shielded her face, ducking like a hungover teenager as she scurried back up the stairs to Wanda's floor. Entering the hallway, the smell no longer bothered her. She'd seen so much, done so much. The smell of rot didn't bother her anymore.

Wanda unlocked her door and the pair of them retrieved the supplies, Tracy balancing the Slim Fast once again on her hip as Wanda rolled the suitcases out the front door. They hustled back down the stairs to the lower parking lot, making two trips with all of the bins and bags.

Tracy beeped the Nissan Leaf unlocked and headed toward it, eyes darting back and forth as she scanned the lot for someone who might cause more trouble. No one appeared. She tugged open the back seat and loaded it up, shoving bags and fully-loaded trash cans into the back until she could barely see out the rear window.

As she shut the door a flash of reddish-orange caught her eye.

Fireball.

He'd run out of the apartment when the fight broke out, the only sensible creature in the room. Tracy crouched on the pavement, fingers out as she called to him. "*Psst, psst.* Fireball, come here, kitty."

She rubbed her fingers back and forth and the little cat eased forward, weaving back and forth as he rubbed himself all over the front fender of the car. "That's it. Come here."

One more motion with her fingers and the cat came within striking distance. Tracy scooped him up and tossed him in the car as Wanda sat in the passenger seat.

"Fireball!"

Tracy slid into the driver's seat and shut the door.

"Oh, Tracy, you found him!" Wanda gave the cat a snuggle before he settled in on her lap. "Thank you."

Without a word, Tracy started the car. Saving a cat didn't make up for the two lives she'd taken. Nothing ever would. But she'd survived. Wanda had survived. Together, they'd make it back to her house, their supplies, and hopefully her husband and daughter.

Tracy backed out of the parking spot, almost silent with nothing but the electric motor. *Please let this car get me home. Please.*

Half an hour later, she had her wish. The drive had been uneventful. No cars on the road. Only a handful of people saw her pass by. She'd kept to the residential streets, only having to back up and turn around a few times. Three days into the end of times and society hadn't gone completely downhill.

Maybe it wouldn't be as bad as she'd feared. Maybe they would survive this without any more carnage. Or death.

Tracy turned into the subdivision and marveled. The neighborhood looked just like she'd left it. Tidy little houses all in a row. Front yards with springtime flowers and green grass. Not a single broken window or dead body in sight.

Nothing like the gated community they had left behind. But looks could be deceiving. Behind all those manicured lawns and swept front porches, her neighbors grappled with this new reality. Not all would take it well.

Tracy wondered how long she'd have before all hell broke loose.

She turned the corner and slowed. *Guess I won't have very long at all.*

CHAPTER TWENTY-SEVEN
MADISON

SACRAMENTO, CA

12:15 p.m.

"FIRST OF ALL, THANK YOU TO THOSE OF YOU WHO came today." Bill cast Madison a glance and she stood a bit taller, folding her arms across her chest in hopes she projected a don't-mess-with-me vibe.

Whatever this man was about, it wasn't anything good.

He rubbed at his mouth before continuing. Was it nerves? His tick for when he delivered bad news?

"I know we all want answers. That's why we're here. Does anyone have new information they'd like to share?"

A murmur swept through the assembled neighbors. The little clusters of people all glanced at each other, furtive eyes darting this way and that. Madison still saw so much hope mixed with denial.

It wouldn't last long.

One man raised his hand.

"Yes, David. What is it?"

The man flashed a brief smile. He couldn't have been much past twenty-five with a close-cropped beard and eyeglasses that screamed hipster. "I still can't connect with any major news outlets. All of my electronics are working since I've got solar back-up, but there's nothing out there besides the emergency alert we've all heard. No one is communicating yet."

"I've tried the radio since it happened and haven't had any luck, either." Madison spoke up for the first time and the whole room turned to her.

"Excuse me? Who are you?"

Madison fought back an eye roll. "I'm Madison Sloane, Tracy and Walter's daughter."

"Aren't you in college?" A woman Madison vaguely recognized asked the question.

Madison nodded. "UC Davis. When the power went out, I hit the road. Got here yesterday."

"The power was out there, too?"

Madison frowned at the sea of expectant faces, no longer surprised, only dismayed. "The power is out everywhere."

A cacophony of questions broke out, neighbors all talking and raising their hands and practically shouting to be heard. The burst of a sharp noise rang out and the room fell silent.

Bill lowered the metal whistle and held up his hands. "Stay calm, please." He addressed Madison. "We don't need to incite a panic, young lady."

She bristled. "That's not what I'm doing. I just thought everyone would already know."

He tilted his head. "Know what exactly?"

"What happened. Haven't you noticed the night sky?" She waved her arm about. "You know, the northern lights? We had a massive geomagnetic storm."

"A what?" Brooke, one of the woman she met walking in, spoke up. "A geo-what?"

Madison wished Tucker was there to explain it. He could do so much better than she could. "I'm not an expert—" Bill snorted as she downplayed her knowledge, but Madison plowed on. "A geomagnetic storm is space weather. The sun emitted a solar flare—that's what disrupted cell service and radios a few days ago."

"I wondered why my reception was so bad!" another man in the crowd said, interrupting.

Madison nodded. "Ordinarily that's all that happens. We lose satellite, maybe cell service because of GPS problems. A solar flare alone doesn't cause any long-term damage. But a massive Coronal Mass Ejection, or CME, followed this one."

Someone else called out. "We don't need a science lecture!"

"We need the power back on!"

A few whispers agreed.

Madison glanced around the room. How could so

217

many grown adults not see the information she had to give was critically important? She frowned deeper.

Was this the future? If people couldn't even stop long enough to hear the truth, what hope did they have to survive what came next? When no one came to help them, what would they do?

Bill called the meeting to order once again. "How about you wrap this up, huh sweetie?"

Madison raised an eyebrow. "I'm not your sweetie. But if you want it wrapped up, fine. You all want to know when the power's coming back on? Try never." She turned around as all the voices picked up, ready to get out of that house and back to the only people in the whole neighborhood who cared.

She made it five feet before a hand wrapped around her arm. *Bill*. He might be twice her age or more, but up close he was still intimidating. His hand squeezed, thick fingers digging into the soft flesh of her bicep. "You're not going anywhere."

"Get your hand off me."

"Not until you tell the truth."

Madison yanked at her arm, but Bill held it tight. "I did tell the truth. The power's never coming back on. The CME caused a massive electromagnetic pulse that killed the grid. It fried every transformer, every power line, every massive piece of electrical equipment from here to New York."

Mrs. Palmer appeared by Bill's side. She reached out and touched his arm. "Bill. Let the child go."

"She's lying. She's just here to cause trouble."

"I am not."

"Why would she do that?" Mrs. Palmer tugged on his arm again and at last, Bill let her go.

Madison took a step back, cradling her arm to her chest. "I'm not lying. The EMP torched the grid. That's why there's no power, no radio, no cell service. It's why the water's out and you haven't heard a single word from the government."

Richard and Tabitha, the couple she had met a few minutes before the meeting started, appeared by Mrs. Palmer's side. "What's going on? Madison, are you hurt?"

Bill waved them off. "She needs to tell the truth and stop spouting this nonsense."

"It's not nonsense." A voice interrupted the commotion and Madison turned to see Tucker and Brianna standing in the doorway.

"Who the hell are you?" Bill advanced toward them, but Madison jumped in between. "They're my friends from college. Tucker's an astrophysics major. He can explain everything a lot better than I can."

Tucker nodded. "It's true. Madison's great at plants, but I'm the science geek."

Bill opened his mouth to protest, but Mrs. Palmer spoke first. "I'll get everyone's attention. They need to hear this."

Madison glanced at Brianna, a question in her eyes.

Brianna shrugged and mouthed an answer. "He wanted to help."

She smiled. *Thank you.*

Brianna held onto Tucker's hand as Mrs. Palmer escorted the two of them up to the front of the room.

"Everyone, please, calm down. This young man is an expert in these sorts of things and he's here to explain."

"Explain what? When's the government coming to help?"

"Why don't we have running water?"

Tucker held up his phone. On the screen was a photo of the massive solar flare that rocketed out from the sun three days before. The room grew silent. "Do I have your attention now? Good."

By the time Tucker finished relaying the events that led to the loss of the grid, the mood in the room had changed from confusion to borderline hysteria. Most people were keeping a lid on it, but Madison could see it on all their faces. They were terrified.

Brooke clung to her neighbor Anna, eyes wide with fear as she pointed back toward her house. Richard and Tabitha spoke with animated gestures, hands flying about as they tried to process Tucker's explanation.

Only Bill stood still, staring straight at Madison.

She suppressed a shudder, clenching her teeth as she stared right back. He wasn't going to intimidate her. No way.

After a tense moment, Bill broke his stare, holding up his hands as he shouted. "Everyone! Everyone! Please be quiet!" He blew the whistle in his hand two more times in rapid bursts.

When the room had once again stilled, he spoke again. "Assuming what this young man says is true, which frankly, I doubt," Bill paused to cast a glance at Tucker, "we should come up with a plan."

People murmured agreement.

"We should assemble a check-in with everyone in the neighborhood. Once we know who's here and who's not, we can move on to an inventory of the houses. In times like this, we need to band together. If someone has more supplies than they need, they should share. If someone has less, they can receive some assistance."

He paused, surveying the crowd. "We can all weather this *temporary* hardship if we pool our resources."

Madison shook her head. He just wasn't getting it. This wasn't temporary. She thought about all the things she'd already seen. The tractor trailer on the causeway. The break-in and shootout at the convenience store.

How much more would have to happen for these people to understand? Would it have to come right up to their door? Would death have to stare them straight in the face?

Tucker and Brianna made their way over to her, the same shock and disbelief in their eyes that she felt inside. Madison couldn't believe this was real. That adults could be so delusional.

She focused on Bill. "This isn't temporary. You shouldn't be giving people false hope."

"You shouldn't be telling people the world is ending without proof."

Tucker held up his phone, but Bill waved him off. "Pictures from the internet aren't proof. For all I know you drew that yourself." His voice rose as he spoke until most of the neighbors had turned to watch. He pointed at Tucker, Brianna, and Madison. "All you've done is show up here and try to incite a riot."

"I'm telling people the truth. That's more than I can say for you. Why do you want to know what everyone has so badly? Are you going to try and steal it for yourself?"

Bill didn't take the bait. "Why are you so reluctant? Do you have something to hide?"

Madison exhaled. She didn't know what to say. Three days ago she wouldn't have hesitated to open her front doors to the entire neighborhood. But after the things she'd seen and done…

Besides, her mother had gathered most of those supplies. She couldn't take it without permission. "You'll have to talk to my mother about that. I can't make decisions for her."

"Oh, I see." Bill advanced, a predatory gleam in his eye. "The minute someone calls you out, now you're just a visitor. That's not really your house, all the things inside aren't yours to give, is that it?"

Bill's lip twitched in an arrogant smirk. "How about all the supplies in that pretty yellow Jeep? I noticed quite a few bottles of water in the back. Were you planning on sharing those, or just rousing up a mob and leaving?"

"That Jeep is mine and so is everything in it," Brianna said. "I'm not staying here and neither is Tucker. We're leaving tomorrow morning."

Bill took another step closer. "Not with all those supplies, you're not."

Tucker took a step forward, the two men separated

by thirty years and Madison's outstretched hands. "Gentlemen, please. We don't need a fight."

Madison waited until both Bill and Tucker stepped back. "Let's go home, have a discussion, and then we'll make a decision. Until then, no one's getting anything."

"I'm afraid that's not acceptable."

CHAPTER TWENTY-EIGHT

TRACY

Sacramento, CA
1:00 p.m.

Tracy slowed the car to a stop to keep from hitting the people streaming out of Mrs. Palmer's house. Everyone was shouting and waving their arms, pointing and talking with exaggerated gestures as they rushed back to their houses.

What the hell happened?

She glanced at Wanda. "What's going on?"

Wanda stroked the sleeping cat on her lap. "I have no idea."

As Tracy stared, a pair of kids darted into the road. One a girl with blonde curls flying away as she ran, the other a boy with moppy black hair that fell in his face. She squinted. *Do I know them?*

She tried to think. Neither was Peyton, Madison's

best friend. Tracy had seen photos of Madison's other friends at school and met her roommate once. Could that be Brianna?

"Oh my gosh, Tracy. Look!" Wanda pointed across the street and Tracy gasped.

Bill Donovan from one street over advanced across Mrs. Palmer's lawn, a shotgun braced across his chest. He carried it with two hands, stalking toward the kids running away.

"What's going on? Were they trying to rob him? Is he going to…"

Wanda's questions petered out as another young woman rushed between them.

Madison.

Tracy's heart lurched inside her chest, a frantic lunge against her ribs, as she caught sight of her only daughter. *My baby.*

Madison held up both her hands, commanding Bill to stop. He raised the gun.

Oh my God.

No!

Tracy grabbed the revolver from the console of the Leaf and pushed open the driver's side door.

"What are you doing?"

Tracy didn't hesitate. "That's my daughter." She leapt out of the car, feet barely hitting the pavement before she was running. No thoughts, only instinct. No plan, only determination.

No one would hurt her daughter. No one.

"Tracy! Tracy!" Wanda's shouts barely reached her

ears. It didn't matter anyway. Wanda could shout the roofs off the buildings and the leaves from the trees. Nothing would get in Tracy's way.

Madison's cheeks flushed red, her hands held out, those gentle palms so defiant and bold. So full of courage, her only child. So strong in her convictions.

Tracy slowed to a walk as she raised the gun. She leveled it right at Bill's face, barrel aiming for the space smack between his eyes. "Lower your weapon."

Both Bill and Madison jerked at the sound of her voice.

"Mom!" Madison lowered her hands, about to rush up to Tracy, but she waved her off.

"Wait, honey."

"Tracy?" Bill asked her name like a question, squinting to look past the revolver in her grip. "What are you doing?"

"Protecting my family. What are you doing pointing a shotgun at my daughter?"

He still didn't lower the gun. Tracy stepped closer, grabbing Madison with one hand and tugging her behind her. "Stay behind me."

Once her daughter was safe, Tracy put her second hand on the butt of the revolver and widened her stance. She wouldn't miss.

This wasn't her first rodeo. That Band-Aid had been ripped clean off already.

"You haven't answered my question, Bill. Why are you pointing that thing at my daughter?"

He scowled. "She came to the neighborhood

meeting to cause trouble. Her and her little friends." As he spit out the words, the shotgun jerked.

Tracy tensed, her finger light on the trigger. "Put the gun down, Bill."

"Or what? You seriously going to shoot me, Tracy?"

She leveled her gaze and took a calming breath. Her words needed to be crystal clear. "Lower the gun. Get the hell away from my daughter and her friends or so help me God, I'll blow your damn head off."

"Mom!"

"Hush, Madison."

"You should listen to your daughter. You're acting crazy."

"I'm not the one standing in the street with a shotgun pointed at some kids half my age."

"They were inciting a panic! They were spouting lies!"

"All we did was tell the truth. No one here knows what happened, Mom. They think the power's coming back on."

Tracy snorted. "It's not."

"You don't know that!" Bill swung the shotgun back and forth, his aim bouncing from Tracy to a spot behind her where Madison's friends must have been standing.

She couldn't let this go on another minute. He was liable to do something stupid. Something he would regret. Tracy took a step forward, the end of the revolver less than two feet from Bill's face.

"What I do know, Bill, is that this won't be the first time I've used this gun today."

Her neighbor's eyes went wide.

"Lower your weapon."

"Come on, Bill. It's not worth it. Just put the shotgun down." Richard Asher, one of Tracy's neighbors from down the street called out from his position on the sidewalk. "No one wants this."

"He's right. Let's all take a deep breath. There's nothing to get violent over." Mrs. Palmer used the most soothing voice, coaxing Bill to stand down.

Tracy wasn't having any of it. They could talk to the bastard all they wanted. She was standing her ground. "I'm only going to say this one more time. Lower your weapon or I will shoot you square between the eyes. You'll be dead before your body hits the ground."

Bill opened his mouth but closed it before he spoke a word. At last, he lowered the shotgun until he held it by only one hand at his side. "This isn't over, Tracy."

She kept the gun trained on his body, but lowered it to point at his chest. "Today it is. You take one step on my property, Bill, and it will be your last." He started to speak, but she raised the gun. "Don't test me. Not today."

Instead of arguing, Bill took a step back, one hand in the air in surrender. Tracy watched him as he turned around and walked back to the sidewalk, falling in step beside another neighbor.

Tracy kept the gun trained on him until Bill rounded the corner and disappeared. Only then did she lower the weapon.

Madison rushed up to her, arms out wide. Tracy wrapped her daughter up in the tightest hug she could manage. "Oh, honey. I'm so glad you're home."

CHAPTER TWENTY-NINE

MADISON

Sacramento, CA
2:00 p.m.

"Will someone please tell me what happened out there?"

Madison glanced up at Peyton with a smile. "My mom went all Linda Hamilton on Bill and threatened to blow his brains out."

Peyton's mouth fell open. "Way to go, Mrs. Sloane! That guy had it coming."

Madison's mom smiled. "Thanks, Peyton. It's good to see you. I'm glad Madison had so many friends with her." She gave Madison another squeeze. "I was so worried about you."

"I was worried about you!" Madison pushed her hair off her face. "I didn't know if you got any of my texts, and then the EMP hit and the power went out. It's been a crazy few days. I didn't know if we'd ever make it here."

"And then when you got here, the house was empty."

"Not exactly empty." Brianna motioned at all the water on the counter. "You did an amazing job getting so many supplies. Even my dad would be proud."

Madison clued her mom in. "Brianna's family is kind of into prepping. You know, preparing for the apocalypse."

Brianna nodded. "It's our thing."

"Well, then I take your approval as quite the compliment. Thank you."

Madison had never seen her mom so tough. Sure, she'd argued with the guy from the county who wanted to dig up the front yard to replace the water meter, and she'd stuck up for Madison whenever she had a problem at school. But her mom never dressed like a commando on a mission.

With her hair pulled back into a tight ponytail and her usual sandals and shorts swapped for jeans and hiking boots, her mom looked so much younger. She had even foregone any trace of makeup. Add in the gun shoved in her waistband, and her mom was a downright badass.

The woman who had been in the car with her mom stepped into the kitchen. Her mom held out her hand. "Everyone, this is Wanda. Wanda, this is my daughter Madison and her friends Peyton, Brianna, and Tucker."

Wanda smiled. "Hello." She held up a pipsqueak of a cat. "This is Fireball."

The cat meowed a hello and snuggled against Wanda's shoulder like it was his favorite place in the world. Everyone took turns giving him a pat before turning to the list of food to eat when.

They all chipped in, with Madison once again teaching Tucker how to work the grill and her mom helping Brianna clean fresh green beans. Wanda set the table with Fireball weaving in and out of her legs.

After they had all eaten, Madison's mom filled her in on the past three days. Madison had a feeling she left out a few details, but then again, Madison did as well. Her mom didn't need to know all the rash decisions they had made and all the risks they had taken to get home.

At last, her mom broached the topic of her father. "Have you heard from your dad?"

Madison shook her head. "Not even once. You?"

"Only once. He texted to tell me his flight was delayed, but that's the last I've heard from him." She reached out and took Madison's hand. "We have to hope for the best. Stay positive. If he can find a way to come home, he will."

Madison nodded. She knew her mom was right. Her father was a fighter. He'd make it home. She turned to Brianna. "Please tell me you're staying the night."

"No one needs to leave. We have plenty. As Madison's friends, you all are welcome here as long as you would like to stay."

Brianna smiled at Madison's mom. "Thanks, Mrs. Sloane. We were planning on driving up to my parents' place outside of Truckee, but after what happened today…" Brianna trailed off and Tucker took over.

"We don't think leaving you all is the best idea. That Bill guy seems like a real hothead. You might need us around."

Madison chewed on her lip. Part of her wanted Brianna and Tucker to stay, but more for the friendship than the body count. But Brianna had family waiting for her. Family who was probably worried sick.

"Whenever you want to leave, it's okay. We'll survive."

"Thanks, Madison." Brianna reached across the table and squeezed her hand as Peyton shifted in his seat.

"As for you," Madison said as she turned to him, "I forbid you from leaving."

"Madison's right. Besides, I hear you'd like a fried pie revival."

Peyton's eyes went wide. "The power's out."

Madison's mom smiled. "Give this Girl Scout a little credit. If I don't know how to cook over an open flame, then I should never have earned that merit badge."

"Don't underestimate my mom's mad cooking skills. If she says she can make a pie, she can make a pie."

"And stick a gun in someone's face!"

Everyone laughed, even Madison's mom. She leaned into her mom, resting her head on her shoulder. "It's good to have you home."

CHAPTER THIRTY

TRACY

SACRAMENTO, CA
   2:30 p.m.

MADISON WAS SAFE. HER FRIENDS WERE WITH HER, they had plenty of food and water and other supplies tucked into the house, and for now, no one was breaking down the door to get it.

Life was as good as it could be. Tracy only wished her husband was there to be a part of it. Every hour that went by, her unease over Walter's absence grew.

She knew that eventually, they would have to leave this little bungalow in the middle of the city. Every day the threats would grow. Whether from other neighbors like Bill, or outsiders looking for an easy mark. The longer they stayed, the more vulnerable they became.

The more she heard about Brianna's family compound in the mountains, the more it seemed like the

233

best option. But they couldn't leave without Walter. He would be coming home, and when he got there, she needed to be waiting.

Tracy thought about sending Madison on her way, demanding that she leave with Brianna and head to safety. But she couldn't bear to do it. For three days she had worried that she would never see her daughter again. She couldn't send her away now.

Whatever happened next, they would face it together. Tracy glanced at all of the faces gathered around her. Four college kids, a librarian, and a fluffy orange cat. Not the most intimidating crew on the outside, but so far they had managed to survive more than she thought possible.

She smiled at Tucker and raised her water glass. "Thank you for warning Madison about the EMP. If it hadn't been for you, we wouldn't be sitting here with all these supplies."

His cheeks colored and he gave her a small nod. "You're welcome, Mrs. Sloane. I'm just glad her text went through."

"So am I." Madison hugged her again. "I still can't believe we both made it home."

"Neither can I, honey." She squeezed her daughter closer to her side. "But I'm afraid this is just the beginning."

Everyone around the table nodded, even Wanda.

"What do you think will happen tomorrow?" Peyton asked the question, his green eyes full of fear and hope.

Tracy smiled. "Tomorrow, I teach you all how to fry

a pie on a campfire and we figure out just what food this cat will eat."

"I vote jalapeño Doritos." Tucker grinned as Brianna punched him in the arm.

"We're saving those, remember!"

"Maybe he'll be a mouser," Wanda offered. "Without electricity, there will be a ton more mice and rats."

Madison recoiled. "*Eww*."

"Hey, don't knock it." Tucker tried not to laugh. "Pretty soon we might be eating them!"

Brianna raised her water glass. "To surviving the apocalypse without eating a single rodent!"

Everyone around the table raised their glasses and Tracy smiled. It might not be the world she envisioned, but the motley band assembled in her tiny home had proven themselves more than capable.

They might have witnessed the end of life as they knew it, but Tracy planned to stick around long enough to see the start of something new. This was only the beginning.

CHAPTER THIRTY-ONE
WALTER

<small>Somewhere near the</small> <small>California-Oregon Border</small>
8:00 p.m.

<small>Walter pulled the tiny compact over to the side</small> of the road. The tires rumbled over the strip warning of his exit, but he ignored them, coasting to a stop in the dust and weeds. He turned the engine off and waited for the headlights to go out.

He stared, dumbstruck.

"So it's true."

He turned to his passenger and nodded. "I guess so." Without another word, he opened the driver's side door and stepped out into the semidarkness.

Instead of dark sky and stars, giant swaths of undulating blues and greens and even purples filled the air. *The northern lights all the way down here.* He rubbed at the back of his neck.

The sky wasn't what bothered him. It was the worrying sight below him that had Walter praying silently for the first time in nineteen years. He had pulled over at the edge of a cliff; one of those lookout spots where tourists could stand and take a photo of themselves in front of an amazing backdrop.

Only instead of the lights of the valley opening up below him, there was nothing but darkness.

A giant, gaping maw, ready to swallow up the beauty of the night sky above it. Had the sun been out, how far could he see? A hundred miles? Two hundred?

There should be lights. Millions of little shimmering lights announcing that civilization lurked just down this mountain. But it was dark, just like he had seen from thirty-thousand feet.

For some reason, he'd kept hoping that as soon as they crested the hill, as soon as they reached California, somewhere, somehow, the lights would be on. But as far as he could see, from Oregon to Idaho and beyond, the lights just blinked out. America sat in darkness.

He thought of the terror down the hill below them. The fear and peril.

The worst was just beginning. How bad would it get? And how soon?

Walter shuddered and turned back to the car.

Hold on, Tracy. I'm coming.

* * *

Want to read more of the Sloane family's story? *Darkness Grows*, book two in the *After the EMP* series, is available now:

FOUR DAYS INTO THE APOCALYPSE, WOULD YOU STILL be alive?

* * *

You can also subscribe to Harley's mailing list for an exclusive companion short story:

www.harleytate.com/subscribe

If you were hundreds of miles from home when the world ended, how would you protect your family?

Walter started his day like any other by boarding a commercial jet, ready to fly the first leg of his international journey. Halfway to Seattle, he witnesses the unthinkable: the total loss of power as far as he can see.

Hundreds of miles from home, he'll do whatever it takes to get back to his wife and teenage daughter. Landing the plane is only the beginning.

Darkness Falls is a companion story to *After the EMP*, a post-apocalyptic thriller following the Sloane family and their friends as they attempt to survive after a geomagnetic storm destroys the nation's power grid.

ACKNOWLEDGMENTS

Thank you so much for reading *Darkness Begins*! I'm humbled and honored that you have taken this journey with me.

If you have a moment, please consider leaving a review on Amazon. Every one helps new readers discover my work and helps me keep writing the stories you want to read.

This series wouldn't have been possible without a hefty dose of faith and support from my family. Post-apocalyptic fiction has been near to my heart for years, but I never thought I would have the opportunity to write it.

Over the past few years, my family and I have grown increasingly aware of the precarious nature of our existence. A single act of terror or a weather event outside our control could change life as we know it forever.

How many of us will be prepared if that day comes?

I hope my books not only entertain, but also inspire the survivalist inside each of us. Being prepared isn't crazy, it's smart.

Until next time,

Harley

ABOUT HARLEY TATE

When the world as we know it falls apart, how far will you go to survive?

Harley Tate writes edge-of-your-seat post-apocalyptic fiction exploring what happens when ordinary people are faced with impossible choices.

Harley's first series, *After the EMP*, follows the Sloane family and their friends as they try to survive in a world without power. When the nation's power grid is wrecked, it doesn't take long for society to fall apart. The end of life as we know it brings out the best and worst in all of us.

The apocalypse is only the beginning.

Contact Harley directly at:

www.harleytate.com
harley@harleytate.com

Made in United States
Troutdale, OR
08/15/2023

12101661R00152